DOCTOR'S O

The Martinis and Chocolate Book Club 1

LARA VALENTINE
Copyright © 2012

Chapter 1

She stood before him with her eyes cast down, her hands behind her back, and her legs apart. She could feel the moisture as it slid down her thighs. She couldn't ever remember being this wet, and she hadn't even climaxed yet.

He reached forward with his hand and plucked at one nipple and then the other, making them small and tight with arousal. Another gush of moisture ran down her legs at the sensation.

"Breathe, slave."

She looked at his hands to see what looked like a small pair of silver tweezers with beads hanging from it. He positioned the tweezers on each side of her nipple and tightened until she gasped at the pain. At her gasp, he slightly lessened the pinch, but it was still tight and uncomfortable. Before she could protest, he quickly did the other side, once again tightening until she moaned and then backing off a little. He gave each clip a tug that went straight to her clit.

"Very pretty, slave. Every time you move it will feel like a pinch from my fingers."

He reached down between her legs and ran a finger along her drenched folds.

"I think you like that. Your nipples appear to be very sensitive. As your training continues, I will find out exactly how sensitive. Now let's continue with your punishment. Crawl over to the chair in the corner and bend over the back of it, resting your hands on the seat cushion."

She dropped to her hands and knees to crawl across the room. With every move of her body it did indeed feel like he was pinching and tugging her nipples. By the time she reached the chair across the room, she was close to orgasm and panting slightly with the arousal. She draped her body over the back of the chair and pressed her thighs together to ease the ache in her clit. The beads on the clips pulled at her nipples, making them ache deliciously, adding to her excitement. She hoped he would let her come soon. She squirmed slightly to find a comfortable position. Luckily, the chair was quite short as she was short in stature. It was also padded so she wouldn't have a bruise from bending over it. She could feel him walking around her, and she hoped she had positioned herself as he had commanded.

"Not quite, slave."

She felt a hard pinch on her thigh and yelped with the pain.

"You are always to keep your legs spread in my presence. Spread them now."

She spread her legs quickly to avoid another punishment. The entire insides of her thighs from slit to knees were covered in her honey. He couldn't fail to notice.

He bent at the front of the chair and pulled restraints from under the cushion. She thought of all the times she had seen this chair and never realized that it was a bondage chair. Soft cuffs were placed around her wrists and then hooked to the restraints. She gave a pull and found them tight. She was definitely not going to be able to get out of this bent-over position. He moved behind her then, and the same soft cuffs were placed on her ankles, which were then clipped to something on each chair leg.

"Lovely. Very lovely."

DOCTOR'S ORDERS

The Martinis and Chocolate Book Club 1

Lara Valentine

EVERLASTING CLASSIC

Siren Publishing, Inc.
www.SirenPublishing.com

A SIREN PUBLISHING BOOK
IMPRINT: Everlasting Classic

DOCTOR'S ORDERS
Copyright © 2012 by Lara Valentine

ISBN: 978-1-62241-432-1

First Printing: September 2012

Cover design by Les Byerley
All cover art and logo copyright © 2012 by Siren Publishing, Inc.

Printed in the U.S.A.

PUBLISHER
Siren Publishing, Inc.
www.SirenPublishing.com

DEDICATION

To all the lovers of erotic romance, this one is for you.

He seemed to like what he saw. She could only imagine what she looked like bent over so lewdly with her ass on display and offered to him for his pleasure and punishment. Her legs were restrained apart so she couldn't press her thighs together against her aching clit and pussy. She knew that from behind he would see her wet and swollen cunt.

He reached between her legs and began to run his fingers through her swollen pussy, drawing moans from her. She squirmed to get his hand closer to her clit. She knew she could come if he would just touch her there.

Smack! *"Stop squirming, slave. You do not have permission to come. This is punishment."*

He stroked the spot on her ass where he had smacked her, soothing the heat.

"Now, for hesitating to obey, you will receive eight strokes and for raising your eyes without permission you will receive two. I will use the paddle today as you are not ready for the crop or the cane. You will count each stroke as the paddle makes contact. For every stroke you do not count, you shall have another. You are not to come. When the punishment has ended I will release you and you will go to your knees and thank me for the punishment. Do you understand, slave?"

She swallowed hard. This was her first real punishment.

"Yes, Master, I understand."

"Good girl. Now what is your safe word?"

"Red, Master."

"At any time, if you cannot take it anymore, you use your safe word. But understand that you are taking this punishment to show your submission to me. Your submission and obedience bring me pleasure. Therefore, punishing you brings me pleasure. What is the most important thing to you, slave?

"Your pleasure, Master."

"Damn! This book is hot." Brianne Templeton grinned as her best friend and fellow book-club member fanned her face. It could have been the book or the Florida heat, but Lisa Hart's face was flushed, and she spoke in a breathless tone. The other women in the book club nodded vigorously in agreement.

Brianne couldn't help but laugh at her fellow clubbers. The Martinis and Chocolate Book Club had been meeting weekly for the last two years, and they had all grown very close. They had named the club after their two favorite indulgences—chocolate and martinis. It didn't take long to add a third—sex. They started out reading all genres of books, but it became clear within six months that they all liked romance, and they all liked it served with a large helping of sex. They liked it even better when that helping of sex was seasoned with some kink. Their tastes were not for the faint of heart. Since then, they could be found every Wednesday reading and discussing their latest selection.

Lisa Hart was their hostess today, and Brianne's best friend. She had met Lisa while working for a local charity, and they had hit it off immediately. Lisa was gorgeous, blonde, and married to a successful attorney. She should have been completely spoiled, but instead she was funny, quirky, and completely down-to-earth.

"I'd let this guy paddle my bottom any day of the week." Lisa's eyes twinkled as she sipped at her drink. She liked the traditional-flavor martini and favored white chocolate.

"I think the idea of a spanking is hot, but actually getting one would probably be a lot different. I don't think I would like to get hurt." Tori Cordell, an old college friend of Lisa's, was just as down-to-earth and alarmingly smart. She drank cosmos and liked dark chocolate. Despite the smile Tori currently wore, Brianne could see sadness and pain in her soft brown eyes. Tori was still recovering from the death of her husband a year ago and adjusting to single parenthood.

"No man is ever going to spank me. But I just might spank one. I wouldn't mind seeing a nicely muscled ass turn red from a paddle or a crop." Noelle Carter laughed wickedly as she sipped at her ice water instead of her usual pomegranate martini and chocolate truffles. She was trying a new diet, and no alcohol was allowed. Her hair was flame red, and that was the most sedate thing about her. She was daring, determined, and a little impetuous. Their eyes swung to Sara Jameson, the only one who had not weighed in yet. She was Lisa's neighbor in their affluent Palm Harbor neighborhood and the newest member of the club. She liked apple martinis and chocolate with sea salt caramel but wasn't drinking today due to her impending motherhood. In her midthirties, she was happily married to a handsome businessman. She was also the quietest of the group and the one to blush the most.

"What? I don't want to be spanked either. Honest!" Sara sported another blush.

Lisa stood and dropped her e-reader on the patio table with a dramatic sigh. "Well, I think this guy is delicious. What do you think, Bri?"

Brianne squirmed in her chair, trying to hide the effect the words had on her. She was very aroused at the thought of submitting, being spanked.

"He certainly is sexy. I like alpha males."

Noelle burst out laughing. "This guy passed alpha in the first Chapter. They don't have a Greek letter to describe him yet." She glanced at her watch and pulled a face.

"Shit. I need to get home and get to work. I have an order due at the end of the week—necklaces for a boutique on Bellaire Beach." Noelle was a talented jewelry designer.

Sara rubbed her bump and smiled ruefully. "I need to get home, too. This baby wants dinner."

Lisa drained her glass and started picking up plates and cups. The women joined in as they discussed next week's selection—a vampire bondage novella. It sounded like another panty dampener.

* * * *

Brianne plopped down on the couch in the living room and propped her feet on the ottoman with a heavy sigh. It had been a long damn week.

"I could sleep for a week, Bri," Lisa groaned as she stretched her legs onto the coffee table.

"Me, too. I swear Kade is kicking my ass on a daily basis. Who knew having a six-year-old and starting your own business would be so much work? Kick-my-ass work." Brianne wriggled her toes and slumped deeper into the cushions. She could hear Lisa's husband, Conor, and the kids playing Rock Band in the family room and wondered where they got their energy. She sure didn't have any left. She swung her legs up onto the couch and picked up the throw pillow to give it a fluff.

"What is this?" Brianne held up a long strip of thick black material that had been tucked under the pillow. She held it closer to examine it and saw that it had Velcro on each end and was padded in the middle.

Lisa jumped from her chair and grabbed for the scrap of cloth, but Brianne pulled it back before she could.

"Is it a blindfold? Holy shit, Lisa, what are you and Conor doing these days? In the living room no less!" Brianne laughed and laughed some more at Lisa's expression. It was hard to embarrass her friend, but it appeared that she had finally accomplished it. Lisa opened her mouth to say something then closed it.

"Come on, Lisa. I don't give a rat's furry ass what you and Conor get up to in the bedroom, or any room in the house for that matter. Considering our reading material, a blindfold is pretty tame stuff.

Lord knows, it's hard enough to keep a marriage hot. I would imagine a little kink now and then keeps him coming home."

Brianne couldn't help the thought that she hadn't been able to keep her own husband coming home. He went home to someone else now. *Fuck! Stop thinking that!*

Lisa held out her hand for the blindfold, and Brianne reluctantly handed it over. Lisa planted her hands on her hips, and a determined expression crossed her face. *Uh-oh, Lisa was pissed.*

"Conor and I have been wanting to tell you this for a long time, Bri, but honestly didn't know how to tell you. It seems that fate has taken it out of our hands, and I'm relieved. Keeping this secret has been difficult, and I don't like keeping secrets from you."

"Secret? You are freaking me out a little bit, Lisa. Are you dying of leukemia or what?" Brianne knew she sounded exasperated, but honestly, what could be that bad?

Lisa sat back down and took a deep breath. "Conor and I live the BDSM lifestyle. He is my Dom, and I am his submissive." Lisa paused as if waiting for a reaction from Brianne. When she didn't get one, she continued. "We have been doing this for about twenty years, since we were dating in college."

Lisa paused again, and Brianne knew she needed to react. She would never judge Lisa and Conor. They were her best friends, had been unwavering in their support since her divorce. It was a surprise and yet not a surprise at all. Lord knew she and Lisa had kinky taste in reading material. It wasn't a stretch that Lisa and Conor had taken the next step and started to live out some of the reading material.

"I'm not sure what you want me to say. I don't care if you and Conor like to get kinky now and then. Really. It's honestly none of my damn business."

"Well, the thing is it's not just now and then. We live this as a lifestyle. We have for many years, and it has been a little difficult keeping it from you since we spend so much time with you. I've wanted to tell you so many times, but I just couldn't find the words."

"Did you honestly think I would judge you? Don't you know me better than that?" Brianne couldn't help the trace of hurt in her voice.

"No! I didn't think you would judge us, but I also wondered if you would feel comfortable around us going forward knowing how we live. I don't want to lose you as a friend. You're my best friend, and I want it to stay that way."

Lisa sat back in the chair with a heavy sigh. Brianne stayed silent, knowing Lisa felt the need to explain.

"One of the guys I dated back in college, he was kind of adventurous. He and I played at a few of the things that you and I have read about. Really mild stuff, honestly. It was Bondage 101. But I knew that I liked it. So when I started dating Conor, I got him to experiment a little, too. We had fun, and we both really enjoyed it. It kind of grew from there, I guess. Then I told Jennifer about it, and she wanted to try it, too. She pushed Nate into it, and he even trained at an exclusive BSDM club as a Dom. When Jen and Nate started living it 24/7, Conor and I started to also. It seemed so natural, we all kind of fell into it. Of course, when the kids came along it became tough to live the lifestyle, but we do the best we can. We feel really fulfilled living this way, and it makes us very happy." Lisa looked cautiously at her, and Brianne was slightly shocked.

"Nate's a Dom? Holy shit, Lisa! Nate does this, too?" Brianne fell back on the pillows.

Lisa laughed. "That's what you got from that explanation? I just spilled my guts about my sex life, and all you hear is that Nate is a Dom!" Lisa laughed until tears ran down her face. Brianne blushed. She had a tiny crush on Lisa's divorced brother-in-law, Dr. Nate Hart. Lisa was constantly trying to push them together, but it was just too soon after her divorce.

"Of course I heard you, Lisa. It's just I had no idea about Nate." Brianne bit her lip as she studied her best friend. "Is Nate going to be okay with you spilling his secret? I don't want him to think I was prying."

"He will be fine with it. We have talked about telling you, and he wasn't against it. He was, of course, worried that you wouldn't want to hang around us anymore, just as we were. But Nate should be proud of his accomplishments. He is an extremely well-trained and disciplined Dom. He gives lessons to other people at the club and is well respected in the BDSM community, not just locally but throughout the US. Subs throw themselves at his feet and beg him to train them." Lisa rolled her eyes.

"We are okay, right? Has anything changed?" Brianne could see the worry in Lisa's expression.

"No, nothing has changed. You and Conor are still my best friends in the whole world." Now that the shock had worn off, she wasn't all that surprised. She felt closer to Lisa than ever. She knew that it was a big deal for them to reveal this to her.

"What about Nate? Do you still want to be around him?"

Brianne was shocked that Lisa needed to ask. "Of course! This doesn't change anything. I like Nate. I enjoy his company, and he is a lot of fun. Nothing has changed. I swear." Well, it had changed a little. Now she would be fantasizing even more about Nate than before. *Oh hell.*

* * * *

Nate Hart held his hand out to Brianne. She and Lisa were sitting on the back patio watching the kids play when Nate had joined them. Brianne gave him a perplexed look.

"C'mon, Brianne. We're going for a little walk."

"I'll watch the kids, Bri. You go for a walk with Nate." Lisa smiled encouragingly at her. Brianne felt a moment of trepidation. Perhaps Nate hadn't been as okay with her learning about him as Lisa said he would.

Brianne placed her hand in Nate's and let him tug her from her chair. It was large and warm, and Brianne couldn't help the tingle that ran up her arm at his touch. He held her hand as they walked down the tree-lined street toward the park at the corner of the neighborhood. Brianne didn't speak and neither did Nate as they strolled toward a bench in the shade. It was already hot and muggy, and it was only ten in the morning. Brianne peeked at Nate's expression from under her lashes. He didn't seem angry. On the contrary, he seemed quite calm. She liked looking at him, she had to admit. He was handsome but not a pretty boy. His dark brown hair was cropped short with just a wave falling over his forehead. His piercing blue eyes were framed with dark lashes any woman would die for, and his jaw was square and strong. At six feet tall, he towered over her, but then just about everyone did. He kept himself in good shape running and playing tennis but wasn't a fanatic about it. He smiled easily and had a relaxed, laid-back personality that seemed to pull people toward him. Well, at least she seemed to be pulled toward him.

Nate laced his fingers through hers and gave her a grin.

"Lisa and Conor tell me you and I are going to have an awkward conversation."

Brianne blushed and hoped Nate would blame it on the infamous Florida heat.

"Seriously, are you okay with this? Lisa said you took the news very calmly and that it didn't make any difference to you. I don't want this to affect our relationship."

Brianne could see that her reaction was important to Nate. She certainly didn't want to tell him about the fantasy she had the night before.

"Really, Nate, I'm fine with it. I would hope you would know by now that I'm really open-minded. As far as weird stuff, this is actually pretty low on the creepy meter, if you know what I mean. It's not like you run about in a red cape and talk to animals."

Nate chuckled. "Well, that's true. I am completely out of red capes, and I gave up talking to animals when they didn't talk back." Nate leaned back on the bench.

"Knowing you as I do, Brianne, you probably have a lot of questions. I would be happy to answer any that you have, if you are curious. In fact, I encourage you to ask any questions you may have. I know about your and Lisa's reading material, so you know some, but books don't always tell the real, or whole, story."

Brianne rolled her eyes and dropped her head into her hands, hiding her face, at Nate's revelation that he knew about the books she liked to read. Nate tipped her chin up so she was looking into his warm blue eyes.

"Hey! There's nothing to be embarrassed about. You're only reading about it. I read about horror, but I wouldn't necessarily want to meet a vampire or a crazed serial killer."

Brianne had to laugh at Nate's analogy. He did have a point, but after all, he usually did. He was smart, and she had always been attracted to very smart men.

"I'm afraid I might ask you something too personal. I'm not sure where the line might be here. This is something pretty personal."

"I'll make you a deal, Brianne. You ask your questions, and if you ask something too personal, I will let you know."

Brianne took a deep breath.

"How did you know you were a Dominant?"

"You mean did I wake up one day and know? Kind of. Jen wanted to try some things she and Lisa had talked about, and I was immediately intrigued. There was no hesitation on my part. When I was at UCLA, me and some of my friends went to a BDSM club. I was floored when I saw what was going on, but I somehow knew it was something I needed to do. Then as I learned more, it was as if a missing part of me was found. I guess I never went through the denial or the shame that some people go through. I need this. It's who I am, Brianne. It's what I am. I couldn't be anything else. I know that after all these years." Nate smiled a gentle smile as he swept her overlong bangs out of her eyes.

"That question wasn't too bad. What else?"

"Do you ever have just regular, um, you know, oh hell."

Nate laughed at her embarrassed expression and stammering.

"Do I have vanilla sex? Is that what you are asking?"

"Um, well, yes."

"Sure. You know how it is when you're married with kids. You can barely get time alone when you are both awake and in the mood. But even when I am having so-called vanilla sex, I am in charge. But please understand that this is not just about sex. A person can be in a Dominant/submissive relationship and not have sex. I have helped train subs for other Doms and not had sex with them. I have dated women since my divorce, had a sexual relationship with them, but not dominated them in the sense you think. I am in charge, but I can only push it so far with them."

"Oh. I guess I just assumed it was all about sex."

"Yeah, most people think that. But Jen was not just my wife, she was my submissive. We had a 24/7 relationship. That means that I was in charge in the relationship, not just in the bedroom. She turned all decision making over to me. I chose her clothes, gave her a daily agenda, and even made the decision about what she would make for dinner. While it was very satisfying to take care of someone like that, it was also fucking exhausting. It was like having a second full-time job. But having a 24/7 relationship was very important to Jen. She needed to serve me. That's how she defined herself. And a Dom's most important responsibility to his submissive, besides always keeping her safe, is to give her what she needs, whether it is what he needs or not."

Brianne couldn't believe that any woman would allow a man to run her life like that. She sure wouldn't, but she would try not to judge. Still, it made her wonder what kind of women attracted Nate's attention. He really didn't seem like the doormat type.

"I thought the submissive was supposed to put her Master's desires first. What she wants doesn't matter?"

"Yes, a submissive should put her Dominant's pleasure and desires first. But a Dom must give his sub what she *needs*, not necessarily what she wants, when she wants it. Think about how fulfilling a relationship can be if each person is focused on the other's happiness. Too many relationships fail because people are focused on their wants and needs, to the exclusion of the other person."

Brianne could see Nate's logic. Certainly, Rick had been focused on himself for most of their marriage. He had rarely thought about what she needed to make her happy.

"Any more questions?"

Brianne gave a heavy sigh and a shrug.

"Probably a bunch, but I think I will chew on those answers for a while if you don't mind. It's pretty cool that you are so open about it."

"I wouldn't say I am open about it. I don't advertise it, but you are a friend. A close friend that I spend a lot of time with. I want to be open with you." Nate gave her a big grin and threw his arm around her shoulders. Despite the heat of the day, Brianne snuggled closer. He smelled amazing. Whatever cologne he wore should come with a warning label.

"Well, you have been. I have had quite the education today."

Nate stood and pulled her up next to him and gave her a big hug.

"Let's get back before they send out a search party for us."

Brianne smiled and finally relaxed. This was Nate. Handsome, smart, easygoing Nate who was such a good friend. Nothing had to be different between them. She just needed to stop fantasizing about him all the time.

* * * *

Nate's fingers tightened around Brianne's. He had been concerned about her reaction. Brianne was open-minded and non-judgmental, but this might have been more than even she could process. Not many people knew his secret, but he had wanted Brianne to know for a long time. He wasn't afraid to admit that she fascinated him. He hadn't been fascinated by a woman in a long time, maybe ever. His relationship with his ex-wife, Jennifer, had started back in high school, but of course he had been fascinated by all girls then.

Brianne was smart, funny, strong, and sexy as hell and the complete opposite of his ex. She was independent, feisty, and didn't take any of his crap. Her submission would be a prize to win. He would have to be worthy to be her Dominant. She would make him earn her submission over and over every day of their lives. And she was submissive. His years of training and his own intuition told him that she surely was. Her preferred reading material aside, she responded to changes in his tone of voice and body language. She also went out of her way to please him, so he made sure to give her positive reinforcement when she did.

She had been through so much with her asshole of an ex-husband that he hadn't wanted to push her into anything she wasn't ready for. Brianne was wary of men, and rightfully so. He knew that the only reason he wasn't lumped in with the rest of his gender was that she didn't find him threatening. He went out of his way to make her feel safe, cared for, and respected.

It was time. He could feel it in his bones. She was ready for a relationship, and that relationship was damn well going to be with him. Now that she knew the truth and hadn't bolted, he would start slowly advancing the relationship. He would start touching her more, invading her personal space, using all the tricks he had learned over the years. He wanted this woman so much.

"C'mon, sweetheart. Let's walk back to the house and get something cool to drink. Man, is it hot out here." Nate tugged her to her feet and slid his arm around her shoulders, pulling her closer than he normally would but not so close that she would freak out. Her body felt soft and warm next to his, and he breathed in the delicious scent—a cross between vanilla and something softly floral. He could feel his cock starting to fill and shifted his stance a little to release some of the pressure. *Down, boy.*

"It is hot, and I need an iced tea. How about you?" She smiled up at him, and his heart beat a little faster as he gazed into her beautiful green eyes.

"Iced tea, huh? I think I will have a cold beer instead, sweetheart."

"Fine. Let's go get you a beer." Brianne laughed as they walked slowly back to the house.

Chapter 2

Brianne didn't have time to feel weird or uncomfortable around Nate. He was at her house for their weekly dinner, as usual. Sunday dinner meant that Brianne cooked and Nate cheered from the sidelines. Luckily, he was an appreciative cheerleader. He always helped with the dishes afterward, too. It never hurt to have a handsome man in the kitchen.

Nate flicked on the music dock, and the sounds of Lady Antebellum filled the room. Brianne smiled as Kade groaned at the music choice from his position in front of the TV. She and Nate liked many of the same songs, but the kids wanted to hear hip hop or rap. Kade was more vocal and raucous than usual tonight. Summer vacation wasn't mellowing him, and Brianne found that all week she had bordered on a headache. Her ex-husband had canceled his weekend with Kade at the last minute, and she had had to deal with an upset six-year-old. Rick had some bullshit excuse about having a cold and not wanting Kade to get sick. The last time he had made this excuse, she found out he canceled to take his blonde, twentysomething wife to Nassau for a long weekend.

She was beyond grateful that Nate had come over for dinner a little early this evening and distracted Kade while she cooked.

"Man, that smells good! I'm starving!" Brianne shook her head as Nate peeked in the oven where her baked ziti was bubbling away.

"Shoo! You are going to let all the heat out." She waved Nate away from the oven and began slicing up the long loaf of bread. The bread would go in the oven as soon as the ziti came out. Nate laughed as he took a draw on his beer. He looked handsome tonight in khaki shorts and a light blue polo that made his eyes look even bluer. His shoulders were broad, and she could see his muscular arms flex as he lifted the bottle to his lips. He had kicked off his shoes at the door, and even his toes were sexy. *Must not fantasize about the hunky Dom in the kitchen.*

"Lisa and Conor are really missing out tonight. Big brother really loves your ziti, almost as much as I do."

"I was in the mood to fix ziti tonight. You know your brother and Lisa have dinner every Sunday night with her parents. They wanted to come when I talked to them, but couldn't think of a legitimate reason to cancel." Unlike Rick who would just make crap up and then do whatever he wanted. *Stop this. Let it go.*

"So, how was your week? You look tired, Bri." Brianne could see Nate's blue eyes soften with concern. She could feel her heart open a little as she looked at him. She didn't have a crush on him because he was handsome, although he was. She had a crush because of things like this. He genuinely cared about her. He was protective but respected her independence. He was solid, and if she wanted to, she knew he was someone she could lean on. After her disastrous marriage, it was almost irresistible. Almost. Her natural fear of getting involved kept her from throwing herself at him. She would never want to embarrass Nate that way.

"Long. Kade doesn't start day camp until next week, so he was home with me. It makes for long days trying to entertain him and still try and get some work done. I have three book covers due next week, and I didn't get much done this weekend either. Rick canceled at the last minute. Apparently, he has a cold." She said the last part with a touch of sarcasm.

"Should I write Dick a prescription? I know how fragile his constitution is." Nate's mouth twisted in derision.

"You writing prescriptions for sinus antibiotics? I don't think even Rick could afford you." Nate was an accomplished and respected orthopedic surgeon. He wore his success casually like a pair of comfortable, faded jeans. He was completely down-to-earth. *If you don't count the whole "he likes to whip women" thing.*

Rick was successful, too. He owned several restaurants in the state of Florida. He also made sure everyone knew how successful he was. When they were married she made the excuse that he was insecure. Now she just called him an arrogant prick.

"Dick has insurance, doesn't he?" Nate threw his empty bottle in the trash and picked up a butter knife to help her smear garlic butter on the bread slices before popping them in the oven.

"Rick is always fully prepared, as you know. And stop calling him Dick. Kade might hear you."

Nate glanced into the living room where Kade was engrossed in a video game.

"Kade can't hear anything, and I just call 'em like I see 'em. He's a dick to you and a dick to Kade. Even my kids know that he's a dick."

Brianne turned away so that Nate wouldn't see the unshed tears in her eyes. Rick's treatment of her didn't bother her anymore, but she wished that Rick could be a better father. He was just too damned selfish. He tried, but he always did something to fuck it up.

She pulled the ziti out of the oven and transferred the bread under the broiler. As she turned, Nate pulled her close for a hug.

"I'm sorry, baby. I didn't mean to pick at old wounds. I just hate to see Kade pay for your ex's immaturity."

Brianne hugged him but quickly pulled back. She should have known she couldn't hide anything from Nate. He seemed to have some sort of superpower when it came to reading her thoughts and emotions. Maybe it was being a Dom that made him that way, or maybe he was a Dom because he was that way.

"It's okay. You know, you didn't tell me about your week, Nate." Changing the subject was a good idea. Dishing up dinner was a good idea, too.

"Kade! Time for dinner!" Her young son rocketed into the kitchen.

"I'm hungry, Mom!" Brianne watched as Nate laughed and ruffled Kade's hair.

"You're always hungry, Jet. Sit down and your mom and I will fill your plate."

* * * *

Nate watched as Brianne padded back into the kitchen. She looked beautiful but tired. He wished he could take some of the burden from her shoulders. She was strong and independent, but no one should have to take on what she did every day. She was a single parent trying to run her own business in a difficult economy. He looked forward to the day when he was allowed to help her. She didn't have to be in charge every minute of the day.

"Is he asleep?" Nate nudged her auburn bangs from her eyes. There were dark circles under them, and he fought the urge to sweep her up in his arms and carry her to bed. He would make her stay there until the circles were gone and her fatigue was lifted.

"Yes, he fell asleep before I even finished the story. All the while he protested that he wasn't tired, of course."

He leaned over and hit the music dock switch and pulled her into his arms. He felt her stiffen against him at first, but the soft strains of Aaron Neville filled the kitchen, and she began to relax against him. He pulled her closer and began to sway to the music, nuzzling her hair and breathing in her tantalizing scent. Her thighs brushed his as she moved against him, leaving heat wherever they touched.

"I love this song. How did you know?"

He chuckled softly as he rubbed his chin on the top of her head. Her hair was silky against his roughened chin. Her hair smelled like vanilla with a hint of some exotic blossom. Since meeting her, he now got aroused whenever he smelled vanilla.

"'Tell It Like It Is' is one of my favorites, too, remember?" He ran his hand up and down her spine, trying to get her to relax with his touch. His campaign to win her had begun. Failure was not an option.

He felt her body melt into his and knew that she had to feel his erection against her stomach. He was tired of trying to hide how his body reacted to her body. Her lush curves were pressed up against him, and his cock was more than happy to rub against her. He pictured her falling to her knees. Her hands would be submissively behind her back, her mouth filled with his cock fucking in and out of her wet, hot mouth. She would suck and lick his hard cock until he came down her throat, swallowing every precious drop her Master gifted to her.

Nate felt her pull back a little, and he looked down into her soft, emerald-green eyes. He could feel the sizzle of awareness running between them, and he felt her shiver as he slid his hand up her spine, across the silky skin over her collarbone, and traced her full, soft lips until they parted. The sultry music washed over him, and he knew he would never hear this song again without thinking of this moment—without thinking of her.

Nate saw the expression on her face change as she started to speak. He wouldn't let her break the mood.

"Hush. You do not have permission to speak." He used his darkest, most commanding dominant voice and was rewarded with her mouth closing and her pupils dilating. She nodded in acquiescence.

He continued to explore her soft lips then ran his fingers across her jaw before tangling in her long auburn hair, wrapping the silky strands around his fingers. He used them to gently tug her head back as he leaned forward to whisper in the shell of her ear, "I think you like it when I'm in charge, Bri."

Before she could respond, he released his hold on her and moved toward the door.

"Sweet dreams, Brianne. I'll call you tomorrow. Lock up after me."

The last thing he saw was her dazed expression as he closed her front door.

* * * *

Sweet dreams, my ass. Brianne rolled over and punched her pillow for the gazillionth time. She was unable to sleep and deep in self-torture, with Aaron Neville playing from her music dock. She would never hear this song again without becoming immediately wet. Her mind couldn't help but drift back to those moments in the kitchen with Nate. He had felt so strong and hard against her. He smelled slightly spicy and musky, and all male. She had wanted to bury her nose in his neck and breathe deeply of his scent.

Brianne remembered the feel of Nate's strong arms around her. She let her fantasies take over from there as the music washed over her already-heated body. He would run his hands over her as if he owned her. She would yield, of course. She knew that would please him.

Her fingers winnowed down into her panties. She was already wet and slick. She began to stroke her clit and imagine what it would be like to be with him. Be his submissive.

His feet came into her line of sight as she stared submissively down at the floor. Her knees were spread wide as she kneeled on the carpet, and her fingers laced together behind her back. Her breasts were pushed forward as if in offering.

"Very good, Brianne. You will suck me now."

His deep, commanding voice made her shiver, and more honey trickled out of her already-burning pussy. She realized he had given her instructions and was waiting.

She lifted her head and saw that his cock was tenting his pants. He had unbuttoned them and lowered the zipper. She reached into his boxers and found his stiff cock. He was long and thick, and her fingers barely wrapped around him. She let her fingers caress his velvety length, and her mouth watered at the thought of it filling her mouth.

She teased him a little with long swipes of her tongue up and down his cock from balls to tip. She swirled her tongue around the head, and his salty taste tickled her tongue. She ran her tongue back down to his balls and laved each, feeling the wrinkles contrast to the smooth skin on his shaft. She opened wide and took as much of his sac into her mouth as she could, sucking and licking while her hand caressed his cock. His fingers tangled in her hair and tugged her to a different angle. She heard his hiss of breath as her tongue found a sensitive spot on his balls.

She moved her tongue back up his cock and engulfed the mushroom head with her mouth while rolling his balls in her fingers. Up and down she moved her head, tightening the seal with her lips.

"Keep that tongue moving. Suck harder."

She moved her tongue faster and hollowed out her cheeks as his hand tightened almost painfully in her hair. She welcomed his mastery and moaned as his cock began to bump the back of her throat. She relaxed her throat and swallowed around his cock. She could feel his balls draw up as she stroked and rolled them. He was close.

She redoubled her efforts, moving up and down even faster, her tongue flicking like a hummingbird with each stroke. She heard his indrawn breath and felt his thighs tense before he shoved his cock to the back of her throat and held it there. His hands tightened in her hair, holding her immobile. He started to pulse, and his hot cum filled her mouth and throat. She swallowed hungrily, loving the salty, musky taste of her Master.

Brianne moaned as her fingers flew faster over her clit. Her body tensed, and her eyes closed in pleasure as her orgasm hit her. Her body bowed and lifted from the bed as pleasure sparked through her.

She slumped back on the bed panting and sated. *Damn.* She hadn't even actually had sex with Nate, and already he was the best she had ever had.

* * * *

It was Saturday afternoon and Brianne was hoping to convince Lisa to hit the mall with her. Kade was spending the weekend with Rick, and Brianne didn't want to spend one more minute at home. She pushed open the front door and headed straight for the kitchen. The minute she walked in she knew something was wrong. The air felt thick with tension, and she stopped short, looking anxiously at Nate. He smiled reassuringly and waved her over to his side.

Despite the strangeness of the last few weeks, Brianne didn't hesitate. Every time she had seen Nate, he had made a point to be close to her. It wasn't anything in poor taste or strange. He would make sure to run his fingers over hers while they were sitting and visiting, or rub her shoulders if she was cooking dinner. He hugged her closely when he greeted her and would kiss her lightly when they parted. It was driving her freakin' crazy. Her crush on Nate had gone into overdrive, and he was on her mind day and night, especially the night.

She was perennially stupid about men, but even she wasn't this stupid. Nate wanted her and was sending her every signal he could. The question was how she felt about it. She adored Nate. He was a wonderful man, and she would trust him with her life. But was she ready to be in a relationship? Was she ready to be in a D/s relationship? She was sure that was what he would demand. The thought made arousal bubble inside her stomach and indecision war in her brain. Right now she was at a "definite maybe" in starting a romantic relationship with him.

"He did, too!"

Brianne was surprised to hear her best friend's loud voice breaking into her thoughts.

"He did not mean to insult you. He just wasn't hungry. Apologize to him right now, slave."

Brianne started in surprise. She had never heard Conor refer to Lisa as his slave. She had heard Lisa call him Master in the weeks since she had found out, but never had he uttered the word "slave." She wondered if being called slave was the BDSM equivalent of a parent calling a child by their first and middle names. She guessed Lisa was in trouble.

"He was insulting!" Brianne almost laughed when Lisa stomped her foot in anger. Her friend was throwing a real grade-A tantrum. Conor looked unamused with a scowl across his handsome features. She glanced up at Nate, and he appeared relaxed as if this was not an uncommon occurrence. Perhaps it wasn't.

"I will not tolerate these tantrums, slave. Nate was simply not hungry. He meant no insult by not eating your cooking. You will apologize. Now."

Brianne had never heard Conor speak with such strength and force. Hell, she almost apologized to Nate, and she didn't do anything. Apparently, Lisa was used to hearing his voice, as it had little effect on her mood.

"No. I won't." Lisa's mouth was set in a mutinous line. Conor glanced at Nate, at her, then back at Nate. Brianne saw something unspoken pass between the brothers before Conor returned his attention to his wife.

"If you will not apologize to Nate, then you will be punished. Either way, you will apologize to him, whether it is before or after your punishment. This behavior will not continue, slave."

Brianne saw Lisa's glare falter a little bit when punishment was mentioned. She glanced at Nate, but his expression gave nothing away. *Damn these poker-faced Doms!*

"Go into the office and prepare yourself, slave. I will join you in a few minutes. Nate, she insulted you. Would you like to participate?"

She saw Nate shake his head.

"No. I trust you to take care of discipline for your slave. The same as you would trust me, bro."

Brianne knew her mouth hung open at the exchange, but she couldn't help it. Lisa was going to be punished? She saw Conor heading up the stairs to the office after Lisa, leaving her and Nate alone in the kitchen.

"I'm not sure what just happened here, Nate."

Nate pushed himself away from where he was leaning against the counter and gave her a big hug as he brushed his lips softly across her forehead. She shivered at his light touch. It didn't take much to make her tingle. His briefest touch could send honey gushing from her pussy. Thank God he didn't realize it.

"It started when I got here. Lisa offered me some of her chicken alfredo, and I said I wasn't hungry. Things went downhill from there."

"You love chicken alfredo, Nate."

"I love your chicken alfredo, Bri. I like Lisa's." A smile played on Nate's lips.

"So you really were insulting her cooking? She's about to get punished and you really were insulting her. That doesn't seem quite fair."

"I was not insulting her. If I had been hungry, I would have eaten it. I was not hungry and said no. She got upset and then didn't leave it alone when her Master told her to. Now she is being punished for her willful disobedience. He gave her a warning, and she did not heed it."

"Still, shit. Is he really going to punish her? He asked you to help him? Where are the kids?"

Nate laughed at her rapid-fire questions, and she blushed a little in embarrassment. She didn't mean to, but it just seemed so surreal.

"The kids are at our parents', same as my kids. Yes, he is really going to punish her. She was pushing him into it, Bri. This was her way of telling him that he hasn't been paying enough attention to her. You know how Conor gets all wrapped up in his work. Well, she made sure he is paying attention to her and only her right now. Believe me, she's happy. She is getting what she wants, and he is, too. As for asking me to help, he invited me to participate since I was the injured party, so to speak. It's just a formality. I have never accepted the invitation. If I did, it would mean administering physical punishment to Lisa. That's not something I am interested in doing. Now, you, on the other hand, are a different story."

Bri's mind seemed to freeze on Nate's last sentence. She had to replay it in her mind before she trusted herself to reply.

"Excuse me?"

"I said that I am interested in disciplining you."

"Say what? Nate, have you lost your fucking mind?" Brianne took a step back and stared into Nate's serious face. But he couldn't be serious.

"No, I have not, and don't swear." Nate's strong arms wrapped around her, and he pulled her close to his warm body. He smelled of citrus, man, and something a little spicy. Her nipples peaked in response.

"We both know where this is headed, Bri. I care about you. I want to be in a relationship with you. I think you have feelings for me, too. I have waited a long time for you. I don't want to wait anymore. You didn't freak out when you learned about me. Now the question is will you freak out when you start to explore this lifestyle. I am betting, big, that you won't. I think you want this, us. This isn't casual for me or for you."

Brianne took a deep breath and exhaled slowly. He was right. She did want him. She was interested in this lifestyle. He was offering her a chance to have both. Did she have the courage to do it?

"I'm scared. This is a lot to take in."

"I know. This is actually a good reaction. I would be worried if you weren't, sweetheart. Do you want me?"

Nate actually looked a little nervous. She couldn't let him think that she didn't want him.

"Yes, I do want you. Very much. But you knew that, didn't you, Doctor?"

Brianne teased him a little.

"I hoped you did. Will you try a relationship with me, Brianne? God, I want you so much."

The last word almost came out as a groan, and he pulled her closer, running his fingers through her long hair.

Well, God hates a coward.

"Yes, Nate. I want to try. I really, really do."

"Ah, sweetheart, you make me happy. You really do. Now let's get go to my house so we can be alone."

So much for a definite maybe. She was at yes.

Chapter 3

Brianne stood in the doorway of Nate's house as he walked through the kitchen and threw his keys on the counter, next to his phone. It was decorated in earth tones with some splashes of greens and blues. She had always found the combination restful, but today it failed to calm her jangled nerves. She was going to have sex with Dr. Nate Hart. She was going to become his girlfriend and submissive. *Holy hell.*

She knew she wanted this with him. She had wanted him for a long time. She had been curious for a long time, too. She had begged Rick to explore their sexuality. Rick had been uninterested in lifting a finger to dominate her. It was just too much effort for her selfish and lazy husband. She closed her eyes to will away the image of Rick's smirk as she had tried to talk to him about their sex life. He had seen her dissatisfaction as something lacking in her. Maybe there was something lacking with her. Maybe she was just one of those women who couldn't feel passion as others did. Maybe she would disappoint Nate. That thought made her start to slowly back out the doorway. *This was a mistake.*

"Stop right there, Brianne."

Brianne froze at Nate's commanding tone.

"Where do you think you are going?"

Back to the car?

"Um, I forgot something in the car?"

Nate strode across the kitchen and caught her hand in his and began pulling her across the kitchen.

"No, sweetheart. There is nothing in the car that you need. Now come here and kiss me. I have waited a long time for this."

Brianne felt Nate's strong arms slide around her and pull her close to his body. He was warm and smelled faintly of soap and citrus. Her nipples pebbled, and her pussy began to cream at the feel of his hard body against hers. It had been so long since she had been in a man's arms. And never had she been with a man like Nate. He was handsome, strong, and good. He made her feel things she had never felt before, and she couldn't help but feel a little nervous.

His hands stroked up and down her spine in a slow, soothing motion. She could feel her bones turning to jelly under his hypnotic ministrations. She let her hands slide up his strong arms, feeling the hard muscle under her palms. His skin felt warm as her fingers trailed up his shoulders to loop around his neck. He had moved closer, and his lips were mere inches from her own. She could feel his warm breath as his lips slowly descended to her own. He stopped mere millimeters from kissing her.

"Do you want this, Bri? Speak now if you don't. I'll take you home and we will never speak of this again. Do you want me? Do you want this? All of this?"

She knew what he was asking. She had to want all of him. She did. She was tired of pretending that she only wanted him as a friend. She wanted him as a woman wants a man. She wanted his dominant side, too. She licked her lips and drew a breath of courage.

"Yes, Nate. I want you. I want all of this. God, I really do."

"Then you will have it, Brianne."

His lips were on hers. His kiss started gentle, which surprised her. She had thought he would devour and dominate her. He nipped at her lower lip and ran his tongue along her bottom lip until she was practically begging him to dip his tongue inside her mouth. His mouth finally sealed with hers, and his tongue began a gentle exploration of her own. She felt his tongue run along her teeth, tickle the roof of her mouth, before sliding against her own. The sensuous foray sent desire coursing through her veins and settled low in her abdomen. She pressed closer to his body and answered his tongue with her own. Her head spun, and her pussy gushed honey as she breathed in his masculine scent. It was an olfactory drug, and she was a junkie. She took another hit of his scent and let it wash over her, pulling her further from her worries and insecurities.

She protested when he pulled back.

"You need a safe word, Brianne."

Nate's words brought her out of her reverie. *Safe word?*

Nate smiled at the look of surprise on her face.

"I don't do anything without a safe word, Bri. Although, if I do my job right, you will never need to use it. You do know what a safe word is?"

Nate arched an eyebrow in question. Brianne nodded.

"Yes, I know what it is. I read about them in my books. I guess I will chose 'red.' That's pretty standard, isn't it?"

"That's fine. It's true, many people use 'red.' I will, from time to time, give you 'yellow,' also. You will use this when you need me to slow down or you need to catch your breath. I will let you know when you have this privilege."

Privilege? Catch her breath?

Brianne could feel more honey trickle from her pussy, dampening her panties further at his dark, commanding tone. She felt very small and feminine as he stood looking at her. He was so tall and strong compared to her petite height. Strong and dominant.

"Go into the bedroom, remove your clothing, and kneel on the rug. I will join you in a few minutes."

Brianne couldn't help the reflex as her hands came up to cover her breasts. She was fully clothed, but the idea of stripping with the lights on was frightening. She had given birth, for heaven's sake. She bit her lip when she saw Nate frown at her actions then give a heavy sigh.

"Your modesty and body image are something we will work on right away. In the meantime, you may leave on your bra and panties for a few extra minutes. Take note, Brianne, they won't be on long."

Before Nate could change his mind, Brianne flew to the bedroom. She didn't think she imagined the chuckle she heard behind her.

* * * *

Brianne's hands shook a little as she pulled her sundress over her head. She carefully folded it and placed it on the dark oak dresser before taking her place on the plush area rug, between the bed and an armchair. Despite the tendency to over-air-condition most homes during the hot Florida summer, the room wasn't overly cool, and she was comfortable in just her bra and panties. She wished she had purchased new ones. The bra was nice enough. She had ample breasts and needed the support after nursing Kade. It was a smooth satin, demi-cup that made her feel a little sexy. The panties, however, did not. She had worn plain white cotton bikini panties. Their only concession to femininity was the lace trim at the top. *I guess they won't be on long anyway.*

She tried to remember the books she had read and what they had said about kneeling. She rested her bottom on her feet and put her hands on her thighs. She was pretty sure she was supposed to look down at the floor. It seemed like forever that she waited kneeling on the rug, when she heard Nate come into the room. He didn't address her but walked over to the closet. She peeked under her lashes and saw him pull what appeared to be a gym bag out of the closet. He dropped it next to the bed and then began pulling the comforter off the bed, tossing it onto the dresser. The top sheet he folded to the end of the bed. He then walked around her and sat in the armchair.

"Look at me, Brianne." His tone was deep and commanding. This was an easy command to obey. She raised her eyes to his beautiful blue ones.

"I am very pleased with how you have prepared yourself for me and how nicely you waited."

Brianne couldn't help the warm glow in her belly that she had pleased him. She wanted to please him more.

"I think your reading has helped prepare you to a certain extent. However, each Master is different in their rules and requirements. I may not do something exactly the way you read about it. Every D/s relationship is about honesty, trust, communication, and negotiation. I will expect complete and total honesty from you, and you will get the same from me. We will communicate our needs and feelings and negotiate the parameters of our relationship. Your job is to trust me completely. Any questions?"

Brianne shook her head.

"It's time to talk about rules. Rule number one is that when I ask you a direct question, I expect you to answer me. I want to hear your answer. Shaking your head or nodding is not considered an answer. So, let's try again. Any questions?"

"No. Um, Sir."

Nate smiled.

"That was a respectful answer, Bri. It pleases me that you want to show me respect. We are in a committed relationship, so it would please me if you addressed me with a title. I would like you to call me Master. Do you think you can do that?"

Brianne nodded and then realized her mistake.

"Yes, Sir. I mean, yes, Master." Her tongue seemed a little tied. Luckily, Nate didn't seem upset. He smiled and ran his finger down her cheek.

"It may take time for Master to come naturally to your lips. It is something that you will work on for me. In the meantime, the most important thing is addressing me with respect. Addressing me as Sir is not going to get you punished. Let's talk about the other rules."

Just the thought of calling Nate her Master had cream dripping from her pussy, and she could feel how her nipples had tightened. If he touched her, she would probably explode. She wasn't sure she had ever been this turned on.

"In a D/s relationship, the slave gives herself to the Master. Your body now belongs to me. Along with it, your pleasure and your pain. When we are together like this, your thoughts, opinions, and wishes no longer count. You are here to serve me and my pleasure. Your only choice is if to use your safe word. What is your safe word, Brianne?"

"Red, Master."

"Excellent, Brianne. Let's continue. When we are together, I expect you to obey and submit to me. You will not question my commands. Hesitating to obey is the same as not obeying at all and will be punished exactly the same."

Shit. That seems harsh.

"You will not speak without permission unless you are asked a direct question. If you need to speak, you will ask respectfully for that permission. I may or may not grant that permission. When we are alone, I expect your body to be open and offered to me for my pleasure and enjoyment. One of the ways you do this is by removing your clothes and having your legs open. You will do this now."

Brianne gave Nate a blank look.

"You will do this now, Brianne. I dislike repeating myself. I want to be patient with you today and give you a gentle introduction into the lifestyle. Consequently, your hesitation to obey will be met with correction, not punishment."

Nate's tone finally broke through her confusion. He wanted her to take off the rest of her clothes, and apparently she had better do it quickly.

"I'm sorry, Master. I didn't understand at first what you were telling me."

She reached back to unclip her bra.

"Ah, I see now, Brianne. If you do not understand a command given to you, you may say, 'Clarification please, Master,' and I will make my command more explicit."

Brianne slid the bra down her arms and then tugged off her panties.

"Hand them to me, Brianne."

She felt exposed and desperately wanted to cover herself with her hands. She had stretch marks on her stomach and thighs from her pregnancy, and her breasts were no longer pert. She had to fight her instincts to keep her hands at her sides. Brianne watched Nate place her bra and panties on top of her dress then kneel next to her on the rug. She could smell the scent of his skin when he was this close, and when he reached out to touch her, she broke out in goose bumps and tingles. She saw Nate frown.

"Are you cold, Brianne? I can turn up the thermostat."

"No! No, Master. I'm not cold. I swear." Brianne blushed when Nate chuckled. He had to realize why she had goose bumps.

"I want to teach you a few things today. The first is the kneeling position that I prefer for you. Rest back on your heels just like that but with your knees spread and your hands laced together behind your back. Look down at the floor about two feet in front of you."

Nate stood while Brianne quickly put herself into position. She held her breath, waiting for his approval.

"That's very good. Just a few adjustments."

She saw the toe of his shoe come into her line of vision as he tapped on the inside of her right knee a few times, then the same on the inside of her left. She slid her knees apart a few more inches. He walked behind her and pressed on the middle of her back slightly so her breasts were thrust forward in offering.

"That's excellent, Brianne. You look very beautiful in this position. I can see I will have you in it often. You may raise your eyes and see how you have aroused me."

She raised her eyes slowly and could easily see the bulge behind his zipper. She couldn't help but wonder if his cock was as impressive as it appeared. She gulped at the thought of it in her mouth or pussy. Honey trickled down her thighs as her body prepared to take him inside. When were they going to have sex? Rick usually pounced on her and would have been done and asleep by now.

"Stand now. I'm going to inspect my new property."

* * * *

Nate hid a smile as Brianne shakily got to her feet. She was a little awkward getting up from the kneeling position, but practice would make her graceful before long. She had done well so far. He could smell her arousal, and it hyped his libido even higher. His cock was hard and painful behind his zipper. She had delicate features with a small upturned nose and full, sensuous lips. She was so incredibly beautiful and sexy, and now she was all his. Her body was curvy and her skin a soft gold tone from the Florida sun. Her auburn hair was thick and long, and he plucked the clip holding her hair back so it fell in waves across her shoulders.

He was finally going to make love to Brianne, and his cock was anxious to get on with it. But like submissives, cocks often had to wait for their pleasure. Today would be one of those days. He wasn't going to rush through their first training session. He would take his time and watch Bri's reactions carefully. She didn't know it yet, but she was going to come many times before the evening was over.

He lifted Brianne's hands and placed them on the back of her head so that they were up and out of the way and her breasts were thrust slightly forward. He could feel her shiver as he ran his fingers down the silky skin inside her arms. He tapped his foot on the inside of each ankle, and her legs slid farther apart. He patted her ass in approval.

"Let's discuss the rest of the rules, Brianne. As I said before, your body, pleasure, and pain belong to me. Therefore, you will not come without my permission. Even when we are not together, I expect you to abide by this rule. Your pleasure comes from me solely from now on, so touching yourself requires my express permission. If you come without my permission, this is grounds for punishment. Do you understand?"

Brianne nodded and then remembered. "Yes, Sir."

Nate could see that this rule didn't cause Brianne any consternation, although she had switched back to "Sir" from "Master." It confirmed Nate's suspicion that her asshole ex-husband hadn't taken care of business at home, so to speak. Her nonchalant acceptance of not coming meant that she probably came very rarely with Rick the Dick. Times would be changing for his lovely slave. He still needed to teach her orgasm control but knew he needed to proceed there cautiously.

Chapter 4

She could feel moisture running down her thighs to her knees. She had never been this wet before. Hell, she was drenched. She had also never been this aroused. She wanted to fall to her knees and beg him to just get on with fucking her already!

His hands, rough from playing tennis and doing yard work but strong and precise from performing delicate surgery, ran along the planes of her face. He didn't speak as his fingers slid from her jaw to her ear and then down her throat, roaming across her collarbone to her shoulders. She squirmed at the light touch and the electric sparks that snapped along her skin.

"Stay still, slave. I am exploring my property. Your only job is to stay still and submit."

"Sorry, Master." Her voice sounded breathless even to her. It was hard to stand still when he was running his hands over her like that. She had fantasized about this moment for so long.

He continued his exploration by trailing his fingers down along her rib cage, tickling her and drawing a giggle that she couldn't hold back. Instead of being angry at her disobedience, Nate smiled.

"Ah, a little ticklish I see. This is important knowledge. If you don't obey me, I can tie you up and tickle you as punishment."

Nate laughed at her fearful expression.

"Not all punishment involves pain, Brianne. Sometimes punishment can involve denial, sometimes too much pleasure can be punishment. Punishment should be designed to fit the infraction."

Brianne couldn't imagine how pleasure could ever be punishment. She could see how denial could be a punishment as he was denying her sex right now. But she could see that he wouldn't be hurried in any way. He was firmly in control.

His hands moved down farther, cupping her heavy breasts. His thumbs brushed back and forth over her nipples, tightening them even more. She had to bite her lip to hold back her moan, and he noticed her predicament.

"Your pleasure belongs to me, slave. You will not hold back your sounds of pleasure or pain. Is that understood?" He pinched her nipples for emphasis.

"Yes, Master." Brianne groaned as pleasure shot straight from her nipples to her clit. She squirmed as a gush of moisture ran down her legs. She felt the urge to press her thighs together to ease the ache in her cunt. She needed him inside her soon. He seemed to feel her urgency as he lowered his head and began to kiss her breathless while his hands roamed her torso. He plucked at her nipples and caressed the sensitive undersides. His hands slid down her rib cage and across her softly rounded belly to grasp her hips while his tongue moved in and out of her mouth. His tongue fucked her mouth while his hands slipped down to her ass and stroked the soft skin. She could feel the moans bubble up in her throat, but they were lost against his firm lips.

He pulled back to look into her eyes, and his fingers slid into her soaking pussy. She heard herself cry out as his fingers slid back and forth along her drenched channel and circled her swollen clit. She tried to move her hips so that he was touching her clit directly, but he removed his hand. She groaned in frustration.

"No, Brianne. You do not control this. I do. Your job is to submit. You will get only what I decide to give you."

Brianne tried to hold still as his fingers began to caress her pussy again. She felt a finger slide inside her, and she moaned as it began to fuck her slowly while his thumb ever so lightly brushed her clit. Her legs began to shake, and she had to lock her knees to keep from collapsing at his feet.

"Oh, Master, please!" Brianne was shocked to hear herself beg yet couldn't bring herself to stop or be ashamed. She needed desperately to come.

"Please, Master. Please may I come?"

She was breathing heavily now, and a fine sheet of sweat covered her skin.

"Soon, sweetheart. Very soon. 'Please' sounds so pretty from your lips. I promise it will be worth it. I am almost done inspecting my new property. Just one thing left." His voice was low and soothing as if talking to a skittish horse.

He leaned over and picked up something that he had apparently thrown on the end of the bed when she was kneeling. The mystery didn't last long as she felt the cold run down her crack. She jumped as she realized what he was going to do.

"Nate! I don't think—" He ignored her infraction of calling him by his name.

"Hush, slave. You do not have permission to speak. Do you wish to use your safe word?" His hands stilled as he waited. Her cunt ached for his touch, and fire licked along her veins. She knew her answer.

"No, Master." She hung her head and closed her eyes in anticipation of pain. She got pleasure instead. He added another finger in her pussy and continued the slow, steady fucking that was driving her quietly insane. She felt him move his fingers, and she caught her breath as he began the slow stroking of what must be her G-spot. *Oh God, so good. Never this good.*

She felt the bulge of his hard cock on her hip as he moved his other hand down her crack and his fingers caressed her tight rosette. He leaned down and began nibbling on her neck while his finger rubbed against her back hole, spreading the slippery lubricant. She didn't realize she was holding her breath until she heard him say, "Breathe, Brianne."

She felt his finger breach her as his thumb brushed her clit. She cried out from the sensation and would have fallen if he hadn't been holding her up. She couldn't hold still as he worked his finger inside her and began to move it in and out, waking nerves she never knew she had. His other hand fucked her pussy and brushed her clit, sending waves of pleasure through her body and curling her toes. Her mind short-circuited with all the sensation and she knew she couldn't hold back another second when she heard his dark, commanding voice.

"Come for me. Come now."

The pleasure seemed to explode from her center, and the waves rolled through her. Pleasure so intense it bordered on pain rode her as she slumped against Nate. Her mind went blank for a moment as the pleasure became consuming. She could feel her pussy and back hole tighten on Nate's fingers. At some point, her arms had come down and she was clutching his shoulders. She threw her head back as he gently bit her neck where it met her shoulder. She heard someone cry out and realized it was her.

The pleasure receded slowly, and Nate wrenched every spasm of pleasure from her with his fingers before he gently withdrew from her swollen core and backside. She felt him lift her up in his arms and place her gently on his bed. He kissed her softly, and she hazily watched him disappear into the master bathroom before returning and lying down next to her and cuddling her close to his big, warm body.

* * * *

Nate's cock felt like it was going to explode. He couldn't remember being this hard or his balls aching this much. He gritted his teeth and recited multiplication tables as he tended to his sexy slave. He needed to keep holding back. She needed cuddling and stroking right now. She had submitted beautifully. She was more than he could have hoped for this first time. Watching her come had been incredible.

He held her as she came slowly back to earth. Her green eyes slid open, and he could see awareness returning. Awareness was good, but too much would ruin the mood. *Time to move on.*

He lifted her arms over her head and with a practiced hand wrapped the soft restraints around each wrist. Her arms were over her head, which thrust her ample breasts up in offering. He could see her frown a little as she tugged at the restraints, testing them. If this was too much too soon, it was time to give her an out. He wanted to push her boundaries but in a controlled fashion.

"Do you need to use your safe word, Brianne? If you need to, everything stops and we talk about it. Nothing bad will happen if you need to use it." He deliberately used her name.

She didn't answer for a moment, and he held his breath until she silently shook her head.

"Words, Brianne. I need to hear you say it. Remember rule number one."

"No, Sir. I don't need to use my safe word." Her voice was soft but sure. He knew he could continue.

"Good girl, Brianne. I am very proud of you. You are so gorgeous when you come. I think I want you to come again."

Before she could react he bent his head and licked her pussy from opening to clit. Her taste was heady, a sweet and musky combination that was all Brianne. She cried out at the touch of his tongue and was soon writhing as he worked his tongue into her hole and tongue-fucked her over and over, pushing in as far as he could. Anchoring her legs down, he ran his tongue around her clit in circles, never quite touching it directly. Her legs were shaking she was so close, and he could feel her clit swelling under his tongue.

"Come, slave. Come for me."

He closed his mouth over her clit and sucked gently. He could feel her spasm as she came, and her cries were music to his ears. He was going to have to make sure she came at least once a day so he could hear them on a regular basis.

He gently flicked his tongue over her clit lightly as her trembling slowed and her breathing became more normal. Kissing a trail up her stomach and up to her breasts, he ran his tongue over her nipples, and she moaned as her body bowed under his ministrations.

* * * *

Brianne's head was spinning, and she couldn't seem to get any words out as Nate began to work his tongue and teeth over her already-sensitive nipples. His tongue circled the taut peak, teasing it even harder while his fingers plucked at the other. She whimpered and was astonished to feel the tingle of another orgasm start. *When was the last time she came more than once in a night? Hell, when was the last time she came with a man?*

She wanted to reach out and touch Nate. His smooth golden skin beckoned, and she could see his muscles bunch as he held himself above her. She tugged at the restraints, but they held her firmly. Nate paused and gave her a grin.

"Don't pull so hard on those, Brianne. If you bruise your delicate wrists, I'll have to punish you."

Brianne felt more honey leak from her pussy at Nate's assertion that she might earn a punishment. She couldn't help but wonder what being punished by him would be like.

"I want to touch you, too, Nate." Brianne gave the restraints another hard tug.

Brianne had barely got the words out before she found herself rolled over on her belly and a large, male hand came sharply down on her ass.

Smack! Smack!

"Ouch! Holy Shit!"

Smack! Smack! Smack!

"How do you address me, slave? And do not swear. You will be punished for that."

Smack! Smack! Smack!

The spanking hurt more than she thought it would, but the heat quickly turned to a blooming pleasure and her clit swelled to attention.

"Master! I'm sorry! Master!"

Smack! Smack! Smack!

She felt herself being turned back over, and her sore ass rubbed against the sheets.

"That's better, slave. As for touching me, you do not touch your Master without permission. Right now, you do not have permission. You must earn that privilege, along with many other privileges."

Brianne didn't reply, as she wasn't sure she had permission to speak, either. The heat on her ass from the spanking cast a glow of arousal that made her want to rub her sore bottom on the sheets. As Nate reached into the nightstand drawer and pulled out a condom, she knew that she wouldn't need to rub against the sheets. He was going to do it for her.

Brianne couldn't help but stare as Nate stood and began to strip his clothes off. His body was firm but not muscle-bound. He looked like a swimmer or a baseball player with broad shoulders and flat abs. Her fingers itched to run all over his body and bring him some of the pleasure he had brought her. He lowered his boxer shorts and his impressive cock sprang out, already hard and glistening with pre-cum. She licked her lips at the thought of his cock running across her lips and tongue.

He stood over her, his expression intense, as he stroked his cock.

"I have been waiting a long time for this, Brianne. This means something to me. You mean something to me. No regrets afterward."

Nate lowered himself over her and lifted her legs over his shoulders. With her hands tied, it left her completely at his mercy, which she was sure he knew quite well. His hard cock started filling her drenched pussy, and she closed her eyes at the exquisite feeling of being stretched.

"Open your eyes. I want you to see who's fucking you."

Brianne opened her eyes and stared into Nate's eyes. They were dark with passion, a darker blue than she had ever seen before. That passion was for her. His face was taut as he held himself in check, entering her slowly. She felt her pussy walls stretch to accommodate his generous size. In her position, she couldn't hurry him along. She could only take what he would give her, when he decided to give it to her.

After he had given her every generous inch of his delicious cock, he pulled back and pumped back in to the hilt in one quick stroke. It rubbed her clit, and she cried out as the sensation ran like lightning up her spine. He pulled out and pumped in again harder, and again it rubbed her clit. She pulled at her restraints, wanting to hold him as he began to ride her hard and fast, each stroke hitting her clit and sending her closer to another climax.

His face was a study in concentration as he fucked her, only changing rhythm to hit a sweet spot inside her that sent her to the edge of orgasm. She could hear his heavy breathing and grunt with each stroke. He must have sensed she was close, and he placed a hand between them and pinched her clit. Stars exploded behind her eyes, and she screamed with the power of the explosion inside her. The waves of pleasure seemed to turn her inside out, and she felt dizzy as he pumped into her one last time and held himself there. She could feel his cock jerk inside her as he came, and she thought she heard him curse as he slumped on her for only a second before rolling off her.

His heavy breathing matched her own as they lay there for long seconds before he broke the silence.

"I just need to take care of the condom, sweetheart. I will be back in a second."

Brianne felt the bed move but was too overwhelmed to register when he returned. She was startled as he untied the restraints and began massaging her wrists and shoulders, cuddling her close and murmuring words of praise.

"You were so wonderful, Brianne. I am so proud of you, baby. Are you okay?"

Brianne roused enough to answer him with a sleepy smile.

"I'm wonderful, Nate. That was amazing. You were amazing."

She could hear Nate's chuckle and feel it, too, as she lay against his chest.

"Well, thank you, sweetheart. I'm glad I have a satisfied customer. Think you might want to do it again sometime?"

It was Brianne's turn to laugh.

"Yes, I definitely want to do that again, Nate. Just as soon as I get some rest."

"I will definitely let you rest, honey. And when you say you want to do it again, do you mean all of it? The restraints, the spanking, and the sex, or just the sex?"

Although Nate sounded lighthearted enough, she could feel the tenseness in his body as he waited for an answer.

"All of it, Master. It was more than I ever thought it could be. I want more."

* * * *

Nate stirred as the first light of the day peeked through the curtains. Brianne's warm body was cuddled against him, her hair tickling his nose. He breathed in her soft scent and felt his cock rise against her soft backside.

Her declaration last night that she wanted more domination and submission, that she enjoyed it, had made him hard all over again. Only the thought that she was exhausted had kept him from flipping her onto her hands and knees and taking her hard from behind. This morning was another story. His pretty submissive was going to get a good hard fucking as her wake-up call.

He ran his hands down her arms, enjoying the feel of her silky skin. He felt her shiver as his fingers trailed over her hips and across the swell of her stomach. His hands traveled higher and cupped her heavy breasts, brushing the nipples lightly with his fingertips. They instantly puckered under the attention.

He lowered his lips to the curve of her shoulder and licked and nibbled a path to the shell of her ear. She squirmed and pressed back against his already painfully hard cock. Two could play at that game. He skimmed one hand down to her pussy while the other toyed with her hard nipple. Her cunt was already dripping, and he dipped his hand into her creamy folds, drawing a moan from his slave. Circling her clit, he bit gently down on her earlobe while giving her nipple a hard pinch. His slave groaned and almost came off the bed.

"Oh God, Nate. Don't stop. I am so close."

She was probably not completely awake, but he couldn't let her get away with that in the bedroom. Time to show her who was in charge when they were in bed.

"I give the orders in the bedroom, slave. Not you. If you want to come, get on all fours."

Nate hid his chuckle as Brianne scrambled to her hands and knees with her heart-shaped ass in the air. He ran his finger down her spine before giving her soft bottom a quick smack. Brianne jumped, and he stroked the red handprint on her milky-white skin. He smiled as he imagined the years that lay ahead of them. They would share a lifetime of love and submission. He would push her boundaries in the bedroom, and she would surely push his out of it.

"If you want to come, grab the top of the headboard and face the wall. You are not to look back, and don't let go. You do not have permission to speak. Now spread your knees a little wider, Brianne. Very good."

Nate leaned down and kissed a wet trail between her shoulder blades and across her shoulders. He grinned as Brianne squirmed a little but didn't turn around or let go of the headboard. *What a good girl.* His lips went down her spine, and he nipped at a pillowy ass cheek before spreading her cheeks and running a tongue around her pink rosette. Brianne groaned at the contact. He heard her pant, could see the honey glistening on her thighs. Her pretty pink pussy peeked out. She was primed and ready. He wanted to play with her all morning, but his cock was demanding that he get balls-deep in her swollen cunt.

He straightened and brushed his cock between her legs and dragged it through her creamy folds. Brianne moaned and wiggled her ass at him.

"Permission to beg, Master?" Her voice was strained and breathless.

"Yes, Brianne. You may beg." Despite his painful arousal, he tried to keep his voice even and controlled.

"Please! Please! Master, please fuck me hard!" Nate could hear the desperation in her pleading voice.

"I love it when you beg, Brianne. Yes, I will fuck you now."

Nate snagged a condom from the bedside table and quickly rolled it on. He held Brianne's hips firmly and sheathed himself in one hard thrust. His eyes almost rolled back in his head at the feeling of her hot, tight pussy caressing him. He began to thrust slowly at first, pulling almost all the way out then pushing back in until his balls slapped her ass. In and out he pumped, building up speed. He rode her hard, lost in the feeling of her pussy, the scent of her hair, and the sounds of their moans. The bed knocked against the wall with the force of his thrusts. He was close, but his good little sub needed to come first. He reached around and caressed her clit before giving it a pinch.

He felt her cunt clamp down on his cock, and she threw her head back and screamed her release. He thrust his cock in one last time and held himself there as his climax clawed out of his body. It started in his balls and ran up his spine and down to his toes. Her pussy milked him of every last drop in his balls, and he pulled out reluctantly, her sensitive tissues causing her to shiver as he did.

When he returned from disposing of the condom in the bathroom, she was still in position, kneeling on the bed with her hands on the headboard, waiting for permission to move. He climbed on the bed and gathered her up in his arms, petting her and crooning loving words. He caught his breath when Brianne looked up at him smiling, love shining in her deep green eyes.

"That was an awesome way to wake up, Doc."

Chapter 5

As usual, Nate didn't have a morsel of food in his house. They decided to head to Brianne's so they could both shower and eat breakfast while they waited for Rick to bring Kade home.

It should have felt strange having Nate in her kitchen that morning. She was kind of dreading the whole "morning after" thing, but it didn't feel strange at all. It pretty much felt like all the other times he had been in her kitchen, albeit this time he wasn't wearing a shirt. He teased her as she cooked his scrambled eggs and toast, making her giggle and almost drop the orange juice. She let him make the coffee. She knew better than to ask Nate to help much in the kitchen. He could repair a torn ACL in an elite athlete but could barely fix a sandwich without something bad happening. He was truly a terrible cook.

She thought he might try to boss her around this morning, too, after the night they had. She was all set to tell him where he could stick his Master-and-slave stuff and had been a little deflated when he completely deferred to her. She ordered him around like a galley slave, and he cheerfully followed her directions, never questioning her once. After they ate, he even waved her off with thanks for a lovely breakfast and offered to load the dishes into the dishwasher. She sat at her laptop to catch up on e-mails, while he cleaned. She could definitely get used to this.

The ring of the doorbell interrupted her reading, and she couldn't help the knot of dread in her stomach as she crossed the living room to answer the door. She knew it was Rick bringing home Kade from their weekend. So far, she and Nate had been wrapped in their own private cocoon. It was about to be ripped away like a Band-Aid off a skinned knee.

She opened the door, and Kade blew into the room, dropping his bag on the floor and running into the kitchen.

"Hey, Mom! I'm hungry!"

Brianne turned to face her ex-husband and his new wife. She couldn't help the annoyance that seeped into her tone.

"You didn't bother to feed him this morning, Rick?"

"Now, Annie, we got busy this morning and didn't have a chance to eat. Tami and I haven't eaten either, you know."

It was all she could do not to roll her eyes. Of course, he would bring the conversation around to himself somehow. As she looked at him, she couldn't tell what she had ever seen in him. He had seemed handsome and charming when they had started dating in college. He was handsome in a pretty boy sort of way, with his wavy blond hair and pale blue eyes. But his chin was weak and lacked character, where Nate's was strong and spoke of integrity. She couldn't understand how he had ever married her either, if Tami was really his type. Of course, basically all women, except Brianne, were Rick's type. She had learned that the hard way in their ten years of marriage.

Tami clung to Rick's arm as if she was drowning. Her brassy blonde hair and heavy makeup made her look older than her twenty-something years. They obviously hadn't been at church this Sunday morning, by the looks of Tami's clothes. She was dressed in denim cutoffs so short Brianne could see the crease where her ass met her thighs. Her lack of bra was obvious under the light pink tank top at least one size too small. You could practically still see the price tags on those tits, Brianne thought.

"I gave Kade a cereal bar to tide him over, Bri. I hope that was okay." Nate walked into the living room with a cup of coffee in his hand. Shirtless.

She almost laughed at Rick doing a double take. She had never seen anyone actually do that and had thought it was just a figure of speech. Apparently not. Rick nodded curtly to Nate.

"Nate, haven't seen you in a while. I don't think you have met my new wife, Tami. Tami, this is Dr. Nate Hart."

Brianne didn't imagine the emphasis Rick placed on the word "new." Tami smiled brilliantly at Nate. Apparently, she liked handsome doctors.

"It's nice to meet you, Dr. Hart. That's Tami with an 'i.'"

"Pardon?" Nate had a puzzled look on his face. Brianne had been through this already when she met Tami and didn't envy him at this moment.

"With an 'i.' My name is Tami with an 'i,' not a 'y.'" Tami looked at Nate expectantly.

"Oh, I see. With an 'i.' It's nice to meet you, Tami." Nate was smiling at Tami politely.

"I wanted something really original, so I changed the 'y' to an 'i.'"

Kade blessedly broke into the conversation before Nate had to reply.

"Can I go upstairs to the spare room, Mom? I want to play video games."

"I thought you were hungry?"

"Not anymore. I ate the cereal bar. Can I?"

"Put your clothes in the laundry room and you can. They are stinking up the living room."

Kade giggled, and Brianne smiled at her handsome son. She had missed him this weekend.

"Dad took us on the boat again this weekend, and we fished. I caught more fish than anyone!"

"I bet you did, honey. You are becoming quite the sailor. Now say good-bye to Dad until next weekend."

"Bye, Dad! Bye, Tami!" Kade tore from the room and up the stairs.

"Well, I guess we should be going. Can we walk you out to your car, Nate?" Rick had a nasty smirk on his face, and Brianne wanted to stomp on his foot.

Nate just glanced down at his bare chest with a smile on his face and sipped his coffee.

"Thanks, Rick, but I'm hanging around here for a while today. But I would be happy to walk you to your car."

Rick's face got a little red at Nate's bland tone.

"No, thanks. We know the way. See you on Friday, Brianne. I'll be here by six to pick up Kade. Nice to see you, Nate. We shouldn't go so long next time." Rick's tone was nasty, and he didn't try and pretend otherwise.

"We won't, Rick. I think you and I will be seeing each other on a pretty regular basis now that I am dating Brianne."

Rick turned and stomped off dragging Tami behind him. Brianne watched them get into Rick's brand-new Escalade before giving in to the peals of laughter that she had been holding back during Nate's exchange with Rick and Tami. Nate just grinned as she laughed until tears ran down her cheeks.

"I'm glad you found that amusing, Bri. You might have warned me about Tami, ya know. What the fuck is with the 'Tami with an i'?"

Brianne wiped tears from her cheeks and leaned against the wall as she caught her breath.

"Tami fancies herself as a pretentious, rich housewife. She did that to me, too, by the way. I, personally, think I handled it better than you did. I told her it was amazingly creative."

"You are a better person than I am then. Dick must be doing well these days. Tami's rack must have set him back about fifteen grand."

"Oh, you noticed that, did you? Yes, he seems to be making money, and Tami seems to be spending it just as quickly."

"It was hard not to notice. Scary, though. A guy could hurt himself they were so pointy. Dick might get gored." Nate smirked.

"Yeah, but it would be nice to be that up and firm or that skinny. Since having Kade I can't claim to be any of that. I guess I am just his smart but chubby, saggy old wife."

Before Brianne realized what had happened the world turned upside down and she was thrown over Nate's knee, staring at the floor.

"I will not tolerate you speaking about yourself that way, Brianne. You will not criticize what belongs to me. Ten for your transgression."

With that, Nate began to smack her ass slowly, counting each one out loud. She wriggled and tried to break free, but his arm was like a steel band.

"What if Kade comes down?"

"I can hear his video game from here. He won't come down here unless you make a lot of noise and fuss. Take your punishment like a big girl so we can continue with our day. Besides, I think this is making you wet, honey. I think you like your punishment."

He was right. The heat of the spanking was spreading through her pussy and making her clit throb. She stopped struggling as he continued the second half of the spanking. Each smack sent spirals of arousal through her, and she whimpered as he gave her the tenth smack and stood her on her feet. She reached back, rubbed her sore ass, and glowered up at him in sexual frustration.

"Stop, Brianne. You are about to say something that is going to get you punished. Again."

She wasn't going to be silenced. Her panties were soaked, and her pussy throbbed in frustration.

"I can't believe you punished me, Nate. We aren't in the bedroom!"

Nate sighed and placed his hands on her shoulders so she was facing him.

"Brianne, listen to me very carefully. I am a Dom. I am always a Dom whether we are in the bedroom or not. I don't normally need to dominate you outside the bedroom, but when I hear you speak about yourself that way, I cannot allow that. You are a beautiful woman who does not need to compare herself with that plastic doll. You are better than that. You are a real woman. Now repeat after me, I am sexy and beautiful."

Brianne could see the seriousness in Nate's clear blue eyes. She took a deep breath.

"I am sexy and beautiful." Nate smiled.

"My Master cannot keep his hands off of me."

"My Master cannot keep his hands off of me."

"My Master loves my body and will keep me well fucked."

Brianne giggled.

"My Master loves my body and will keep me well fucked."

"Very good, Bri. I can smell your arousal. But you will not have release. The frustration will be a reminder of this lesson, so it will not be repeated."

Brianne's smile vanished and she opened her mouth to speak, but his finger silenced her before she had a chance. Nate used his darkest Dom voice.

"No, Brianne. Don't say something we will both regret."

Brianne pressed her lips together and fought back her frustration.

"Good girl. You are learning. Now let's have a wonderful day. By the way, very good girls will get release later tonight."

She was going to be as good as gold.

* * * *

His hands trailed down from her high cheekbones, over her throat, until he was cupping her full breasts. She drew in a deep breath as his thumbs brushed her nipples. They tightened in response along with her drenched pussy. She desperately wanted his cock inside her, filling her, driving into her. She pressed herself closer, and she heard him groan as his cock pressed into her belly. His length was impressive, and she lowered a hand to rub him through the fabric of his jeans.

"Stop that, baby, or this is going to be over before it begins. I want to come inside that tight pussy, not my damn jeans."

She laughed with the heady feeling of power and rubbed faster.

"Wouldn't it be terrible if we had to start all over again?"

"Witch!"

Before she knew what was happening, he had lifted her up and thrown her down on the bed, hovering over her, the look in his eyes almost feral, his white fangs peeking through his smile.

"Do you think that's what he really wanted to call her?" Noelle laughed as she sipped her peppermint martini, her diet long abandoned.

Tori popped a truffle into her mouth and sighed. "Why would he call her a bitch? She's about to put out."

"Well, they all put out eventually." Lisa laughed.

"I love vampire stories. They seem so dashing, a little less alpha than the werewolf stories." Sara sighed, rubbing her swollen tummy. She was close to her due date.

"Don't you like alpha males, Sara?" Lisa asked. "I sure do love me an alpha male."

Sara shrugged. "I like them okay. But I prefer charming to steamroller. I want to be romanced, not mated."

Brianne smiled. "I don't know about that. I am really beginning to appreciate an alpha male."

Lisa grinned. "Yeah, I just bet you do. Seems like my brother-in-law is taking good care of you these days. You've had a goofy smile on your face for weeks."

"What?" the other women screeched in unison.

"You're dating Nate? Holy shit, Bri. You never even mentioned it. How long has this been going on behind our backs?" Tori's hands were on her hips, and her foot was tapping impatiently.

"I wouldn't say it was behind anyone's back. We haven't been hiding it. In fact, Nate strolled in front of Rick completely shirtless in my living room."

Noelle whistled. "Oooo, Nate shirtless. Hot damn!"

Brianne scowled playfully at Noelle.

"Hey! That's my boyfriend you're sitting there fantasizing about."

Noelle chuckled. "Well, good for Nate. Rick deserves a little payback, the asshole. And good for you, too. About time you moved on, and Nate seems like the perfect person to move on with. We always knew he had a thing for you."

Lisa rolled her eyes. "That's a major understatement. He freakin' worships the ground she walks on."

Brianne blushed a bright red. The last few weeks with Nate had been some of the best of her life. Despite his demanding schedule, he still made sure he spent time with her and with Kade. He was the epitome of the alpha male but not a prick about it. He felt safe and strong, a haven when her life got a little too crazy.

He had been telling the truth. He was a Dom all the time. But he didn't feel the need to push her around to get his way. He was respectful of her feelings, and she found that he was more than willing to negotiate as long as it didn't have anything to do with her safety or body image. He wouldn't budge an inch there. She had been the recipient of two more spankings before she realized that criticizing herself would not be tolerated. Otherwise, he seemed content to let her have her way pretty much all the time.

The sex. Oh the sex! It just kept getting hotter. She had come more in the last three weeks than she had in the last three years. He was totally in charge in the bedroom, and that was just fine with her. She trusted him completely. She had never even thought of using her safe word, had never needed to. He seemed to know when and how to push her boundaries to bring her the utmost pleasure.

She was so horny lately that it seemed as if she was wet all the time. She fantasized about him all the time and she was not allowed to bring herself off without his permission. He had yet to provide that permission no matter how much she begged and pleaded in texts or over the phone. Even now, she was squirming in her chair, wet and aroused, not from the reading but from her memories of the night before.

"I certainly do worship her." Nate's deep voice startled Brianne, and she turned in surprise to see Nate and Conor strolling onto the patio.

"I thought you were watching the kids, not spying on us," Lisa teased Conor.

Conor smirked and leaned down to kiss his wife and whisper something in her ear. Whatever it was made Lisa turn a rosy red.

"My fault, Lisa. I stopped by after my last surgery to see if Brianne wanted to go to dinner and a movie tonight."

Nate pulled Brianne up from the chair, sat down, and the resettled her on his lap. Brianne saw the faces on the other women, and they looked positively tickled. *Why not throw them a bone?*

"I missed you today, Nate." Brianne leaned down and brushed her lips over his.

Nate's eyebrow quirked up in surprise. She barely had time to register his quick grin before his lips came down on hers. His mouth owned hers, and his tongue delved into her mouth, staking claim. She felt shivers go down her spine as he leisurely explored her mouth with his tongue, seductively rubbing her tongue with his own and tickling the roof of her mouth.

He lifted his lips and whispered into the ear softly, so no one else could hear, "I missed you, too, slave. I have plans for you tonight."

She almost came just from the kiss and his voice alone. She vaguely remembered that she was sitting in a circle of her closest friends with a man's tongue down her throat. She pulled back and peeked through her lashes at the amused and some downright-envious faces of her book club.

"Holy crap on a cracker, girlfriend! Have a little pity on us single gals who aren't getting any." Noelle groaned and rolled her eyes.

"Sorry, um, I guess we got carried away." Brianne could feel Nate's chuckle in her ear.

"You can carry me away anytime, Nate," Noelle teased.

"Sorry, Noelle, I am too busy worshipping this beautiful woman."

Brianne's friends practically swooned. She turned back to Nate's soft blue gaze.

"I don't think I can go tonight. I have Kade. Rick canceled on us. Again."

"Handled, honey. Kade is chomping at the bit to spend the night here with Lisa and Conor's kids. My kids are at Jen's tonight."

Brianne's, Lisa's, and Nate's kids had grown up like siblings, so spending the night at each other's house was a normal occurrence. It was many of the things she loved about their friendship, but she couldn't help but be especially grateful at this moment. But she didn't want to give in too easily.

"Lisa, are you okay with having one more tonight? I don't want to impose."

Lisa laughed off Brianne's concern. "After my three, I won't even notice one more. But if it will make you feel less guilty, you and Nate can watch ours on Friday night. I have been wanting to see that new romantic comedy."

Conor groaned pitifully at Nate. "Say no, man. Don't make me go."

Brianne smiled mischievously. "We would be happy to return the favor, Lisa."

Conor eyed Brianne, and his lips twitched. "I think I need to have a talk with Nate about not letting you walk all over him. He needs to stand up to you, Bri."

Something in Conor's look made her gulp and glance at Nate, who was rubbing his chin in thought. Yep, she was in so much trouble.

Chapter 6

Nate threw his keys next to his cell phone and began flipping on lights through the house. Brianne couldn't help but admire the way his khaki shorts hugged his firm ass and his T-shirt clung to his broad shoulders. She would be happy entering a room behind him anytime.

He had surprised her with a romantic dinner at a local restaurant on Clearwater Beach. Afterward they decided to skip the movie and walk off dinner instead. They dug their toes into the sugar-white sand and watched the gentle waves of the Gulf of Mexico. Like many Florida residents, Brianne was too busy working to make a trip to the beach very often. She had forgotten how relaxing it was. She could have listened to the water for hours.

Nate flipped on the last light and turned to pull her close to him. She breathed in his delicious scent, citrus and something else, burying her face in his shirt.

"Do you want to play a little, Bri?"

Nate's voice tickled her ear, and her nipples tightened in response. She nodded affirmatively, rubbing her face against his strong chest.

"Then go upstairs and prepare yourself. You know what I want."

She certainly did. It was what she wanted also. She practically ran up the stairs and into his large master bedroom. There was no reason to run. He would give her plenty of time, but she was looking forward to this, to tonight. Between her son, and his son and daughter, they didn't get much alone time. She pulled her shorts and shirt off, neatly folding them and placing them on the dresser. Next came her bra and panties, also neatly folded on top. Last to go was the clip that held her long auburn hair off her neck. Nate liked it down and free so he could tangle his fingers in it.

She picked up a pillow, threw it on the floor, and knelt on it facing the chair. She relaxed into the pose, back straight, hands laced together behind her, knees wide, and eyes down. Now she would wait. He always kept her guessing. Sometimes she would wait only a few minutes, other times several. As time ticked by, she could see tonight would be the latter.

When he finally came in she held herself still, not giving in to the temptation to look up. She heard him moving around the room, making preparations, she was sure, for their evening. She heard the lighter, and then the scent of candles wafted through the room. Another click and the ceiling fan and light turned off. The room was bathed in soft candlelight and a delicious vanilla fragrance.

"This scent always reminds me of you, slave."

She felt Nate's fingers stroking her hair. She almost purred in contentment and pleasure. She could feel her pussy starting to cream in anticipation of the pleasure Nate would bring her.

"I am very pleased with how you have prepared yourself for me. Tonight I am going to push your boundaries a little bit. If at any time you want to stop, you say your safe word. What is your safe word, Brianne?"

"Red, Master."

"Good girl. Let's begin then."

* * * *

Nate's cock was already painfully hard against the zipper of his shorts. One look at Brianne kneeling so submissively and his cock had stood at attention. He had hardened further when she had continued to be still while he prepared the room. Now he knew he would never make it through the evening he had planned unless he took the edge off a little. He stroked Brianne's silky hair before tangling his fingers in it and gently but firmly turning her face up to his.

"I think you will show me oral service to start this evening off, slave."

"Yes, Master."

Nate quickly shed his clothes. It really wasn't fair of him to come first like this, but he was just too far gone to be able to hold back. He would make it up to her later with two orgasms for his one. He stood before her and spread his legs a little. She lifted up and took his balls in her left hand, caressing them, while her tongue snaked out and licked him from root to tip. His eyes almost rolled back in his head at the sensation. He knew he wouldn't last long. He started reciting multiplication tables in his head to hold back and enjoy the pleasure.

Her soft pink tongue laved his balls, and then she opened wide to suck one into her mouth, scraping her teeth gently over him. *Holy shit.* He had taught her exactly how he liked to be sucked, and she had proved to be a star pupil. By the smile on her face, he could tell that she knew that at this moment it was she who was firmly in control. She might be the one on her knees, but she was the boss.

He tangled his hands in her hair to try and get some control back, but she chose that moment to suck the head of his cock in her mouth while flitting her tongue over the underside. He groaned as he realized that he had completely forgotten to continue reciting multiplication tables and his balls had drawn up, ready to explode.

Her head bobbed up and down, and the gentle suction combined with her torturous tongue had him teetering on the edge of orgasm. He could feel the climax start in his lower back and the pressure start to build with each stroke of her warm tongue. Her mouth felt like a hot, wet glove, and he gave up trying to hold back.

He groaned one last time, and his fingers tightened in her hair, holding her head in place, his cock in her hot mouth. The climax exploded from his balls and almost sent him to his knees. He spurted his cum into her mouth and watched, mesmerized, as she greedily swallowed every drop he gifted to her. She licked him clean and then sat back on her heels, waiting for his next command. She had a ghost of a smile on her face. The little witch knew that he was trying to fucking pull himself together after her devastating mouth and tongue. He shook his head a little to free himself from his daze and get the scene back under his control.

"That was excellent, Brianne. You have pleased your Master. We will continue now. I have many plans for you tonight."

* * * *

Brianne sat back in satisfaction knowing she had literally rocked Nate's world. The intense look on his face right before he came had amped up her own arousal. She was wet and swollen, and she desperately wanted to press her legs together to ease her throbbing clit. She knew that would not be allowed.

"Look at me, Brianne."

Brianne looked up into Nate's eyes. They were dark blue with desire and—dare she even think it—love?

"I think you need to be shown just how much I worship you, Brianne."

Brianne watched as Nate reached into his bag and brought out cuffs, which he efficiently wrapped around her wrists and ankles. He ran his finger around each, making sure that the cuffs weren't too tight. He brought her wrists behind her and clipped the cuffs together before pressing on her back so her shoulders and face were pressed against the floor and her ass was in the air. He reached into his bag again, and she could hear him opening a package.

"Stay in that position, Brianne. I need to give this new toy a quick wash."

She heard water running, and then Nate returned and knelt next to her. His hands ran up and down her spine, and his mouth followed the same path, sending sparks to her already-tingling pussy. He kissed and nibbled her ass cheeks, and she could hear his chuckle as she squirmed in position. He spread her ass cheeks apart, and she moaned as his tongue explored her back hole. It poked and tickled, and she felt her cream dripping down her thighs and could smell her own arousal.

She jumped a little when the cold lube drizzled into her crack. Nate held her down with a firm hand at the small of her back. His probing finger at her ass was not unexpected. He had been exploring her forbidden hole since that first night, patiently using his fingers to stretch her. She had experienced anal sex before, with Rick, but had never enjoyed it. Rick had never prepared her, and all she had felt was embarrassment and pain. With Nate, it was completely the opposite. His patience never ceased to amaze her when it came to this or anything else. Perhaps he got this from being a surgeon?

She felt one finger press into her, more lube, and then a second finger was added. Her body shook as he moved his fingers in and out, scissoring them and stretching her tight entrance. She felt the pinch and then the burn and a frisson of delight ran up her spine and down to her toes. She whimpered when he removed his fingers, but they were quickly replaced with something else pressing against her hole, demanding entry.

"Breathe, Brianne, and press back against the plug."

Brianne took a deep breath and pressed back against what felt like a log trying to gain entrance to her ass. She felt him begin to fuck her very slowly with it, and she pressed back with each thrust, becoming bolder as the slight pain changed to pleasure. He gained a little more ground each time, added more lube, and continued pistoning the plug in and out of her ass until it slid in to the hilt. Her breath came out in a hiss as she tried to become accustomed to the pressure of the plug. His hand patted her bottom in praise.

"Good girl, Brianne. I am very proud of you. Tonight, I am going to fuck this ass as is my right as your Master. The plug will make it easier and more pleasurable for you when I do."

Brianne shuddered and almost came hearing the dark promise in his words. She had known this was coming, just not exactly when. They had discussed this possibility, as they discussed everything, and she had assured Nate she was open and eager for this experience with him. She knew that if she had expressed even the slightest hesitation this wouldn't be happening, no matter how much he talked about a Master's rights.

Strong, warm hands helped her to stand, and she lowered her gaze to the floor, her hands cuffed behind her back, legs spread, waiting for his next command. His hands cupped her chin, tilting her face up for his kiss. His firm lips came down on hers, and his tongue demanded entry. Her knees went weak as he slid his tongue sensuously along hers, sucking it into the cavern of his mouth. He lifted his head and nipped at her bottom lip before soothing it with his tongue.

"I have a gift for you, Brianne. A token of my worship."

Brianne heard Nate rummage in the bag, and then his feet were back in her line of sight.

"Look up, Brianne."

Brianne looked at, and her eyes fell on the glittering objects in Nate's hands. They appeared to be chandelier-style earrings with green and blue beads. He held them up for her to inspect.

"Nipple clamps that I had made just for you. These are emeralds for your eyes and sapphires for mine. They symbolize our bond as Dominant and submissive. I hope you enjoy wearing them as much I will enjoy seeing you wear them."

Holy shit! They were emeralds and sapphires? What was Nate thinking? She couldn't even wear these out to dinner. Could she? The thought of wearing them under her clothes in a public place made her blush with excitement.

"What thoughts just went through your head? They must have been good ones from the blush you are sporting. You can tell me later. Let's see how these look on you."

He leaned down and took first one then the other nipple in his mouth, sucking and licking until they stood at attention. She bit her lip in anticipation of how these would feel. She had read about them, but she was going to experience them firsthand.

She watched as he placed what looked like tweezers on each side of her nipple and pushed up the gold ring, tightening them until she made a noise of pain. He immediately backed the ring down just a smidge before quickly attaching the other clip to her nipple. She once again groaned at the pain, and he backed off again. The clamps were tight, and she licked her dry lips, unsure how to react to the foreign feeling of her nipples being constantly squeezed.

"Breathe, Brianne."

She slowly took a breath and then another.

"Tell me how it feels. Do they hurt?" His fingers caressed the delicate undersides of her breasts.

She was about to say yes, but it wasn't really the truth anymore. The pain was morphing into the most delicious pleasure. His fingers were caressing her breasts, and his hand would brush the beads, causing the clamps to tug slightly on her nipples. The sensation went directly to her clit, and she moaned as he gave the beads another swipe.

"No, Master. They don't hurt." Brianne could barely get the words out, the pleasure was so intense.

"I asked you to tell me how they feel, Brianne. You will do this now." His hard, commanding tone brooked no refusal.

"Tight, Master. Like you are pinching and tugging them."

"Does this excite you?" He brushed the beads again, sending sparks from her nipples to her clit.

"Yes, Master. It excites me very much. Thank you for the gift." She almost groaned the answer.

Nate smiled tenderly down at her and continued brushing the beads back and forth.

"I'm glad you like my gift, Brianne. And what a sweet slave you are to thank me for it. My worshipping of you is not complete, of course. Come here, sweetheart."

Nate led her to the end of the bed and faced her toward the top of the bed. She was standing in front of the footboard of his massive four-poster bed. He unclipped her wrists and massaged her shoulders. Her head lolled back as he kneaded her muscles.

He reached for something at the top of the high finial, raised her right arm, and clipped her wrist to a restraint. He moved to her left side and quickly did the same.

"Spread your legs wide, Brianne."

She slid her legs far apart, and he restrained her ankles to the bottom of the bedposts. She was left standing in an X position with her arms restrained to the top of each bedpost and her ankles to the bottom, her feet planted firmly on the floor. She tugged on each restraint, but there wasn't much give. He had restrained her well. His hand glided up her back and tangled in her hair, tugging her head back so she was looking in his eyes.

"You cannot imagine how beautiful you look restrained here for my pleasure. One more thing."

He reached into his bag and brought out a black strip of fabric. Brianne knew what this was—a blindfold. He wrapped the thick cloth around her eyes, blocking out the subtle candlelit room. Her other senses came alive, and she could smell his scent, feel his breath on her neck, the brush of his hands as he fastened the blindfold snugly.

"Do you need to use your safe word, Brianne?"

Ah, her sweet Nate. She wouldn't use her safe word for all the money in the world right now.

"No, Master. I don't need my safe word."

"Good girl. Let the worship continue."

* * * *

Nate lifted her hair, breathing in her scent. His cock was already hard again at the sight of Brianne restrained so beautifully, just for him. The nipple clamps decorated her breasts, and he couldn't help but reach over and give each of them a gentle tug. A moan escaped from her soft, full lips.

He began kissing her neck where it met her shoulder then trailed those kisses down her back, circling her heart-shaped ass. He tugged at the plug that was snug in her ass, jiggling it, and smiled to himself as Brianne tugged at the restraints, her breath coming in pants. She liked that more than she wanted to admit, he was guessing. He knew she had experienced anal sex with Dick, and that experience had been sadly lacking. He was determined that only pleasure would come from her experience with him.

He dropped to his knees, kissing the backs of her thighs while playing with the plug.

"I am on my knees in worship, Brianne. You're the only woman in the world that can bring me to my knees."

He breathed in the heady scent of her arousal and licked at the honey that coated her inner thighs. No doubt that Brianne was on the edge, and he did owe her one. He reached between her quivering thighs and ran his hand along her drenched slit. Damn, she was wet. It wouldn't take much for her to go over. He teased her entrance then moved his fingers to her hard and swollen clit. He circled it over and over, finding a rhythm until her body was strung taut like a bow.

"Come now."

Brianne threw her head back with a scream, and cream gushed from her pussy, drenching his fingers. She pulled on the restraints frantically, a light sheen of perspiration covering her golden skin. He lightly stroked her clit until every spasm had been wrung from her body and she hung limply from the restraints. It was time to take her down, but he wasn't finished with her yet.

* * * *

Nate's strong hands held her up as he released the restraints from her ankles and wrists. She steadied her legs, but he was already guiding her to the bed, placing her on her knees and pressing her shoulders down into the mattress. He pulled her right wrist back and clipped it to the cuff on her right ankle, repeating the process on her left side. The clamps on her nipples tugged downward, sending sparks outward and down to her pussy. She could feel herself start to build toward release again at the submissive position Nate had placed her in. His inventiveness seemed to know no bounds, and she delighted in his creativity in the bedroom.

He pushed her knees wider apart, and she felt him begin to nibble the inside of her thighs, his tongue tracing erotic patterns on the delicate skin. She shivered in arousal as his tongue found her swollen cunt, already sensitive from her orgasm, tongue-fucking her opening. She moaned at the sensation and bit her lip to keep from begging for another climax. She ground her head into the mattress as his tongue laved her pussy and lightly feathered over her clit. She cried out in frustration when his tongue abandoned her.

"Not yet, Brianne. But soon."

The first smack of his hand on her ass startled her, but the pleasure bloomed quickly sending sparks of arousal from her warm ass to her hot, needy cunt. Each smack on her ass added to the overall warmth, and she wriggled trying to incite him to spank her more. With each stroke, the plug shifted in her ass, sending her excitement ever higher. When his hand struck her pussy, she cried out, at first with pain and then with pleasure. She slid her knees a little farther apart to expose more of her sopping cunt. He took the hint and smacked her pussy once, twice, three times. The third smack, just hard enough to sting, sent her over and she screamed as her climax hit her hard. White light behind her eyes would have blinded her if she hadn't already been blindfolded. Wave after wave of pleasure radiated from her pussy through her entire body, almost painful in its intensity.

She heard the crinkle of a condom wrapper, and then his hard cock brushed her warm ass cheek. He pressed his cock into her, and she was so wet, so ready, he slid in to the hilt with one strong thrust. His hands anchored on to her hips, and he began powering in and out of her, his balls slapping her ass with each stroke. His cock felt huge with the plug in her ass, stretching her pussy. She started the inevitable climb to another orgasm with each thrust of his beautiful cock, so his abrupt retreat made her wail in protest.

"That's not where I am going to come tonight, Brianne. I am going to come here."

He tugged lightly on the plug and began to work it slowly out of her tight hole, tossing it aside. Her ass clenched at the empty feeling. She needed something there. She felt his cock line up with her back hole and a rush of cold as more lube was poured in her crack. He pressed forward into her tight star. His cock was larger than the plug, and she felt the now-familiar pinch and burn as he slowly filled her ass. His cock rubbed against sensitive nerves, and she panted and moaned until he was completely inside her. She could feel the crinkly hairs on his legs brush against her thighs. His own breathing was ragged, and she could feel his tense control in the tightness of his muscles. He was waiting for a sign from her that he could move. She took a few deep breaths and swayed her ass just slightly from side to side.

She could hear his exhale, and his cock began to piston very slowly then built up speed. She moved with him, inciting him to fuck her harder, faster, just not stop. Her release built quickly, and she was beyond the ability to speak, to beg. They moved together, completely in sync, driving toward an explosion. Her brain barely registered his voice, whispered into her ear. "Come, Brianne."

Nate reached around and removed a clamp from each nipple, the blood rushing in painfully. She screamed as her orgasm overtook her. Colors flashed, and she gulped air as her body tightened painfully, then released, only to be repeated over and over. She felt Nate thrust into her and hold still, grunting his own release. His cock jerked inside her backhole as he came, long and hard, his hands biting into the soft flesh of her hips. She might have bruises tomorrow, but tonight she didn't care. The feel of his hands on her body only amplified her arousal, and she gave herself completely over to him, glorying in his dominance.

As she came down from her climax, Nate gently pulled out of her and disposed of the condom. With gentle hands, he unclipped her wrists from her ankles and removed her blindfold. She stretched out on the bed while he massaged sore muscles from her toes to her shoulders. The bed moved, and she was starting to fall asleep when she felt him lift her up in his arms and carry her toward the master bath.

"What's going on? I was sleeping, Nate."

His chest rumbled against her cheek as he laughed.

"I know, sweetheart. But you may be very sore tomorrow. A nice soak in the Jacuzzi tub will ward off some of that."

She felt him lower her in the steaming, swirling water, and she felt her whole body relax. He took such good care of her. She had never known a more nurturing man. He joined her in the tub, pulling her back against his chest, not forcing her to talk. He allowed her to just be for a few minutes before she felt the need to communicate with him.

She ran a finger down his muscled arm. "That was amazing, Nate."

Her voice was barely a whisper, but she knew he heard her. He kissed the top of her head and nuzzled her neck.

"That's a major understatement, baby. You blew me away tonight. I don't feel worthy of such sweet submission, but no one else is either, so I'm going to take it."

She chuckled and burrowed deeper into his arms.

"You're right. No one is worthy, but you come pretty damn close."

He growled at her words. "I think you came several times, Bri."

He turned her so she faced him, his face somber and serious suddenly.

"I love you, Brianne. I have for a while but didn't want to scare the hell out of you. I'm not taking this back. I love you so just deal with it. I want to spend my life with you. So what do you say about that?"

Brianne traced his strong jaw with her fingertips, feeling his past-five-o'clock shadow.

"I love you, too, Nate. I am scared. I won't deny that. But I love you, more than I thought I could ever love a man. And you damn well better want to spend your life with me because if you think you are doing this stuff with any other woman, you are sadly mistaken."

Chapter 7

Brianne sat at her design table working on a book cover when she heard Nate's car pull into the driveway. They had been together three months now, and Brianne could easily say this was the best time of her life. The best time but not an easy time. Nate was strong and opinionated, and she was, too. They were learning what buttons were a bad idea to push on each other and which were a good idea. So far, they had many more good buttons than bad.

Nate rapped on the door before coming in.

"Oh my God, what smells so good in here?"

Nate dropped his briefcase at the door and was pulling her out of her chair to kiss her hello.

"Well, you could be talking about the lasagna in the oven or you could be talking about my perfume."

"You always smell nice, baby, but I didn't eat lunch today, so I'm talking about the heavenly smell from the kitchen."

Nate followed the smell all the way to the oven, peeking inside before Brianne had to shoo him away with a sigh.

"Stop opening the oven. You always open the oven, and that lets the heat out."

"I'm starving, honey. How long until dinner?"

"Half an hour, give or take. Tide yourself over with a cookie. I made a fresh batch of oatmeal this afternoon."

Nate grabbed two off the platter, bit into one, and closed his eyes in ecstasy.

"I would love you for your cooking alone, Bri."

"I don't know what you did before you dated me, Nate. I'm surprised you didn't starve."

"I just ate a lot of fast food or bummed a meal from Lisa and Conor. Since dating you, I've gained five pounds."

Brianne ran her eyes over Nate. It sure didn't show. His middle was still trim and lean.

"Worried about your girlish figure?"

Nate popped the rest of the cookie in his mouth and gave her ass a smart smack.

"Ouch! Shit, Nate!"

"Don't tease the mean Dom, Bri."

Brianne rubbed her bottom and stuck her tongue out.

"You never learn. I'll show you how much I appreciate that behavior later tonight."

Nate reached for another cookie, and Brianne was just about to slap his hand away when she heard the doorbell. Finally! Rick was bringing Kade home today after two weeks of their summer vacation. She almost knocked Nate over getting to the door.

"Whoa, baby! Where's the fire?"

"It's Kade!"

Before she could get to the door, it opened and her son ran in, practically mowing her down with his little body. She laughed as she knelt down and hugged him close. She had missed him so much. The house wasn't the same without her little man. She rained kisses all over his face until he wriggled away.

"C'mon, Mom! That's enough. I'm too old for this. Tell her, Nate!"

Nate chuckled and hugged Kade for himself.

"You're on your own with Mom, Jet. She really missed you. If I were you, I would let her get those kisses out of her system."

They both looked up as they heard someone clear their throat. Rick.

He stood in the doorway with a strange look on his face, as if he was lost.

"Come give your old dad a hug, Kade. I won't see you for a while."

Kade turned to hug Rick, and Brianne couldn't help but notice that Rick held on to him until Kade wriggled free from him, too. Maybe Rick was finally figuring out that this time with Kade was precious. She could only hope.

"Well, I need to go. Tami is waiting in the car. I hope you had fun on the boat this week, Kade. Be a good boy and listen to your mom."

Brianne gaped at Rick. Since when did he tell Kade to listen to her? He was usually rolling his eyes and telling her she was overprotective and old-fashioned. Rick handed Nate Kade's bags and waved at them before hurrying back to his car.

"That was weird." Nate stared after Rick with narrowed eyes.

"I'm not going to question it. I spent too many years trying to figure out why Rick did anything. I am done. Kade, let's get your bags upstairs."

"I'll do it, honey."

"Thanks, Nate. Throw the dirty clothes in the laundry room and I'll start the washer in a few minutes."

Brianne shook her head as she thought of Rick's strange behavior. Maybe he was finally growing up.

* * * *

Brianne pulled the garlic bread out of the oven and threw the pot holders on the counter as she yelled up the stairs.

"Boys! Dinner!"

Nate came halfway down the stairs.

"Honey, I think you need to come up here."

Geez, what now? Brianne ran up the stairs after Nate.

"Are all his clothes stinky again? I think they spent most of their time on the boat."

"Well, yeah. But that's not what I wanted to show you. This is."

Nate swept his arm toward the bed. Brianne's eyes widened in amazement. The bed was covered in new toys. There was a tablet computer, a Nintendo DS, video games, an Xbox, LEGOs, action figures, and stuffed animals.

Brianne rubbed her eyes, but the pile of swag didn't disappear.

"They're mine, Mom!"

Kade's little chin, so like her own, was set in a determined line.

"I am not questioning that, sweetheart. But where did you get all this stuff?"

"From Dad. He said he wanted to buy me some stuff. He picked it all out."

Kade sounded defensive, and she knew he was afraid she was going to take it all away.

"He picked all this out, Kade?"

"Well, most of it. I picked out the LEGOs and toys. He wanted to buy me this stuff! He said he wouldn't see me for a while and wanted to get me some new toys."

Brianne rubbed her temples and gave Nate a wry smile. Her ex-husband could give her a headache quicker than anything or anyone.

"Okay, I will take this up with your dad. But in the meantime, I am going to put some of these toys away for later. We can discuss which ones after dinner. Now it is time to eat. I will call your dad afterward."

Brianne gave Nate a grim look as they headed downstairs. Her hope of Rick growing up appeared to be optimistic.

* * * *

Brianne hung up the phone a little harder than she needed to. She was pissed. Specifically, she was pissed at Rick. Leave it to him to shower expensive gifts on her son and then refuse to pick up his phone when she tried to call him about it. She had been trying him for the last two hours, and he wasn't answering. She knew it was bullshit. He kept his cell phone on him 24/7 and usually had it sealed to his ear. The fact that he hadn't answered meant only one thing. He was avoiding her. He was avoiding her and doing a damn good job of it.

"No answer?"

Nate walked downstairs and drew her in his arms. He smelled like heaven, spicy and masculine. She snuggled into his arms and laid her head on his chest where she could hear his heartbeat.

"No, the asshole is screening his calls. I left voice mails, but I don't think he wants to talk to me about this. Thank you for reading to Kade, by the way."

"No problem, sweetheart. I know you needed to deal with this issue. Why do you think Rick did this?"

"Who knows why Rick does anything? Guilt, maybe? He seemed to be reluctant to let Kade go earlier. Maybe in his own twisted way he is trying to make it up to Kade. That's how Rick used to deal with our issues. He would buy me something. He thought that made it okay."

Nate rolled his eyes. "It would be cheaper to just be a nice guy."

"That was always Plan B for Rick."

* * * *

His hands were tangled in her long, dark tresses, using them as leverage as he rode her hard and fast from behind. He untangled his right hand and gave her ass a sharp smack, leaving a red handprint starkly outlined on her satiny white skin. She moaned and pushed back to meet his thrusts, urging him on, pushing him to fuck her faster and harder. His hand came down again and again, leaving her ass bright red and her begging him to touch her clit. Anything to let her come. His face was a mask of grim determination as he ignored her ragged pleas for release. He continued to spank her, pistoning in and out, finally reaching around—

"Shit! Who could be at the damn door?" Brianne scowled at the sound of the shrill doorbell.

"Just at the good part, too." Lisa smirked at the other women in the club.

"I dunno. This guy seems like a real asshole. I wouldn't let him touch me." Noelle laughed.

Brianne opened the door and smiled as she recognized her neighbor from down the street. "Sam! How great to see you! Please come in. Can I get you a cup of coffee? It's fresh."

The handsome man gave a sheepish smile as he entered her living room.

"I am sorry to intrude, ladies. Brianne, I would love a cup of coffee, but you should know that this is not strictly a social call."

Brianne gave Lisa a quick glance. They both knew what Sam did for a living.

"I'll make him a cup of coffee, Bri. How do you like your coffee, Sam?" Lisa offered.

"Touch of cream, one sugar. Thank you very much."

Lisa disappeared into Brianne's kitchen while she settled Sam on the sofa.

"I hate to disturb you, Bri. But something has come up, and well, I volunteered to come over here to talk to you about it since we're friends and neighbors."

Brianne leaned forward. She didn't like the look on his face at all. Sam looked around searching for something.

"Is Kade here?"

Brianne felt panic rising in her throat.

"Is this something to do with Kade? Has he been hurt?"

"No! No! I'm sorry. I didn't mean to suggest that anything had happened to Kade. I take it he isn't here?"

Brianne shook her head, concern written on her features.

"He's over playing at a friend's house while I have my book club here."

"Good, I really don't want to discuss this if Kade is in the house."

Brianne huffed in exasperation.

"So far, Sam, you haven't discussed anything."

"Damn, I'm sorry. I swear I am not usually so inarticulate, but I think this news is going to be something of a surprise, so I am just going to say it straight. Rick has run off to the Cayman Islands. He cleaned out all his business accounts and left his business partner high and dry."

Brianne's mouth hung open in shock.

"He and Tami left the country? Oh my God."

Sam shifted uncomfortably in his seat.

"Well, that's another thing. He didn't flee the country with his wife. Apparently, he fled with one of the servers from his restaurants—a Mike Taylor. We know they flew from Tampa International to the Caymans, but we have lost their trail from there. They have probably picked up new identities and are traveling under assumed names. Oh, thank you."

Sam reached up for the coffee from Lisa. Brianne tried to take in Sam's words, but one word kept getting in the way.

"He ran off with another *man?*"

"Yes, according to the letter he left his wife, he and this man had been seeing each other for quite a while. They left to start a new life. Unfortunately for Linus Elliott, he took everything with him."

Brianne knew Linus well. He had been Rick's business partner for years, and she thought he had always been a nice man. She couldn't believe that Rick would leave Linus with nothing after all they had been through together.

"Are you sure, Sam? Rick's an asshole, but he was never a criminal."

"Yes, I am sure. I'm sorry, Brianne. That's why I wanted to be the one to tell you."

Brianne looked around her living room at the grim faces of her friends. Everything was coming clear now. Rick's behavior made a hell of a lot more sense. He had known he was going to leave, and his spending spree was linked to his departure. How like him to think that possessions could make up to Kade for not having a father. For the millionth time she wondered how she had ever ended up marrying Rick.

"I'm afraid I need another favor, Bri."

"Of course, Sam. You know I would do anything to help the police find him."

"I appreciate you feeling that way." Sam sipped at his coffee as if reluctant to ask his favor.

"Can you come down to the station and answer some questions? You might know something that you don't even realize that you know. It might lead to recovering the money and bringing Rick back."

"Is she a suspect?" Lisa jumped to her feet.

"Absolutely not. But she was married to Rick for many years, and she knows a lot about his habits. She might be able to help us."

Brianne rubbed at her temples again. Rick was becoming a permanent headache.

"Okay, I want to help. Do you want me to come now?"

Sam stood gratefully.

"That would be wonderful, Bri. I can drive you there and bring you home afterward. I appreciate this very much. I really do."

Lisa picked up her cell phone and frowned.

"I'm calling Conor, Bri. He can meet you there. You shouldn't talk to them without an attorney. Promise me you won't."

Sam had the grace to look a little embarrassed.

"I promise I won't, Lisa." Brianne grabbed her purse and keys.

"Sorry, we can't finish the meeting tonight, ladies. Lisa, can you pick up Kade at 6:00? I don't know how long I will be."

"Sure, honey. Are you going to call Nate?"

Brianne shook her head. "Not right now. He said he would be working late, so I don't want to bother him. I'll talk to him tonight."

Lisa looked troubled. "Bri, I think you should call Nate. He would want you to."

"I'll call him later. I would only get voice mail right now anyway. C'mon, Sam. Let's get this over with."

* * * *

Brianne sipped at her soda and rubbed her aching temples. If she ever saw Rick again, she was going to kick his ass from here to kingdom come. She had been answering questions for over an hour, and she wasn't sure that anything she said was going to help them find Rick or the stolen money.

It wasn't that she didn't want to help. She really did. Upon her arrival at the police station, she had seen Linus coming out of the interrogation room, looking pale and grim. He had seen her and given her a big hug. He murmured all the right things when you haven't seen someone for a long time and probably wouldn't have ever seen them again if circumstances hadn't thrown them together again. Still, Linus was a good man and shouldn't have had to go through this.

Conor had shown up at the station minutes after she did, and he didn't look much happier than Linus. Conor had never liked Rick much but had kept his mouth shut while she was married. After the divorce, he had taken the gloves off and made his feelings clear. He gave her hand a squeeze now in encouragement. This interview seemed to be taking forever.

"Did any of Rick's business contacts ever come to your home?" Sam's partner was going down what looked like a checklist of questions and thankfully appeared to be close to the end.

Brianne shook her head. "Rick didn't like to mix business with his home time. He was on his cell constantly, but he never brought people to the house. Nor did I ever accompany him when he met with people. I'm so sorry I can't help you."

Sam's smile was forced. "It's okay, Bri. One of your answers may lead us to him. You never know."

Conor placed both hands on the table in front of him and leaned forward in an aggressive stance. He hadn't been in a good mood the entire time.

"Are we done here, Sam? Brianne is exhausted and obviously shocked at was has happened. She has to go home and face her six-year-old son and tell him that Daddy has left the country with his lover and is on the run from the law. If you have any more questions, you can contact my office and I will relay them to her."

Both the officer and Sam nodded in agreement. They looked exhausted, too.

"If we have any more questions, we will contact your office, Mr. Hart. Thank you for coming in, Brianne. We do appreciate your time."

"I'm just sorry I couldn't be more helpful."

"No worries, Bri. We have an interview with Mrs. Templeton right after you, and she may have some information that can help us."

Brianne looked at Conor in surprise. They hadn't talked to Tami yet?

"I would have thought the first person you would talk to would be his current wife."

"We had some trouble getting a hold of Mrs. Templeton to schedule some time with her."

Brianne blinked in confusion.

"Tami didn't make the report to the police?"

"No, Linus Elliott did. Mrs. Templeton called him when she received the letter. Mr. Elliott brought the letter to us when he made the report. He said that Mrs. Templeton was extremely upset by the news."

Brianne couldn't help but feel sorry for Tami at the moment. Despite how she felt about Tami, she did seem to really love Rick.

Conor helped Brianne out of her chair and led her through the door to the hallway. Tami was sitting in a chair, texting on her cell phone. Brianne's heart went out to her when she saw Tami's swollen, red eyes. She had obviously been crying.

Sam addressed Tami. "Mrs. Templeton? We are ready for you now. Can you come with me?"

Tami tucked her cell phone in her Louis Vuitton bag. "You can call me Tami. That's Tami with an 'i.'"

Brianne didn't wait for poor Sam's reply as she let Conor lead her down the hallway and to his car.

Chapter 8

The minute Brianne opened her front door she knew her long day was about to get even longer. She had to tell Kade about Rick. Thankfully, Nate was playing a video game with Kade, and they were sitting on the floor in front of the TV laughing and talking trash to one another. Nate looked up when she closed the door.

"Where's Lisa?"

"Lisa went home after I got here. I told her I could watch Kade."

Brianne blew out a breath as she gazed lovingly at her son.

"Thanks, Nate. It has been a long day. How was your day, sweetheart?"

She ruffled Kade's hair and gave him a big smile. Kade shrugged.

"It was okay. Nate and I were playing video games, and I was kicking his butt. Where have you been?"

Brianne glanced at Nate. He had the same grim expression that her friends had worn.

"I had to go talk to someone. Are you hungry, baby?"

"Nope. Nate made peanut butter sandwiches, and we had chips, too. You never make me peanut butter sandwiches for dinner. How come?"

"Well, gosh, I don't know, honey. I'll have to think about that. Did anything catastrophic happen in the kitchen, Nate?"

Nate rolled his eyes at Brianne's not-so-subtle dig.

"You can check for yourself, but nothing exploded or broke. I even cleaned up after myself."

"I believe you. You are very good about cleaning up after me. Kade, let's get your bath done, sweetie."

"Awww! Now, Mom? I was winning!"

"Yes, now. Let's get your bath over with."

She looked into Nate's sympathetic eyes.

"Go get ready and I will be there in a second, baby. Scoot."

Brianne nudged Kade toward the stairs. He hated bath time until he was actually in the bathtub. Then she couldn't get him out of it.

Nate pulled her into his arms as soon as Kade was out of sight. He rubbed his hands along her shoulders, kneading the tense muscles.

"Oh, man, that feels good. I have to tell him, Nate. I can't keep this from him. I am so fucking tired of cleaning up after Rick. He makes a mess, and I clean it up."

She felt his hands slide into her hair and knead her scalp. It felt so good her knees almost buckled. What did she do to deserve this man? *Put up with her scumbag of an ex, that's what!*

"Well, sweetheart, if I ever see Dick again, I will be more than happy to kick his ass for you. And then I will kick it again for Kade."

She groaned as his fingers dug into her scalp, and she felt a little of her tension start to recede.

"You'll have to wait in line after me, Lisa, and probably Tami, too."

"I'll wait until after you, baby, but I want some of his scrawny ass left to kick. I won't wait until after Lisa and Tami. Especially Lisa, she knows how to kick butt."

She rested her head on Nate's chest. She could feel his heart beating. Just the sound seemed to relax her a little.

"I better go give Kade his bath. Then I am going to have to tell him, Nate. Fuck, this sucks."

"If you want me there, Bri, I will be. I don't want to intrude, but I would like to be there for you."

Brianne was acutely aware that she hadn't called Nate when everyone had told her that he would want to know. She felt pretty shitty for leaving him out. He had heard about all this from Lisa. He should have heard it from her. *Shit.* Being in a relationship was hard.

"I'm so sorry, Nate. I should have called you. I meant to but things got away from me at the police station. I didn't want to leave this kind of voice mail on your phone. Are you pissed at me?"

Brianne peeked up through her lashes to check out Nate's expression. She was surprised to see it was one of sadness, not of anger.

"No, sweetheart, I'm not angry. Just disappointed that you didn't feel strongly that you could share this with me. I can't help but wonder if you feel that you couldn't trust me to help you through this."

Now she felt even worse. His disappointment was much harder to take than anger.

"No! I do trust you. I swear. I would trust you with my life. With Kade's life, too. I guess—I guess I am just used to handling things on my own. Rick was never there to help me, so I just had to deal with things myself. It's a hard habit to break."

Nate traced her jaw with his fingertips.

"Do you think it is a habit worth breaking, Bri? I want to be there for you. I want you to be there for me, too. I want us to be a team."

Brianne hugged Nate tightly.

"Yes, yes, yes! It is a habit I want to break. I want to be there for you, too."

"Mom! Are you coming upstairs or not?"

Nate and Brianne both laughed at Kade's phenomenal timing and extremely healthy lungs. Brianne decided to show Nate that Kade got those lungs from her.

"*Yes!* I'm on my way right now!"

Brianne could hear Nate laughing all the way up the stairs and into the bathroom.

* * * *

Brianne crawled between the covers after her terrible, crappy day and practically draped herself over Nate. She just wanted to sleep and wake up in a world where the last twelve hours hadn't happened. She had just had the worst conversation of her life, and that included when Rick told her he was leaving her for a twentysomething blonde waitress. This had been much worse. She would rather cut off a limb than have her son hurt in any way, especially by a man that was supposed to love him.

With Nate by her side, she had broken the news to Kade as gently as she could. She left out the part about leaving his wife for his lover but left in that he had broken the law. Kade needed to understand that even if Rick came back he was in a great deal of trouble. She had tried to assure Kade that his father loved him and that this had nothing to do with him. But when Kade's bottom lip trembled and his green eyes filled with tears, she knew that nothing she said was going to make this okay.

"Bri, we can talk to a friend of mine. She's a child psychologist and may have some advice. You may also want Kade to talk to her."

Brianne sighed as Nate's warm hands stroked her hair.

"Yeah, that's probably a good idea. One conversation couldn't hurt, and I'll do anything to help him through this."

"You are a wonderful mother, Bri. Kade is so lucky to have you for his mom. Now what are we going to do about you?"

"Me? What about me? I got over Rick leaving a long time ago."

"Not Rick leaving, Bri. The feeling that Rick has taken control of your life right now."

"What, are you some kind of psychiatrist, Nate?"

Nate rolled Brianne onto her back, pinning her there with his big, strong body.

"No, slave. I am your Master. And as your Master, I am supposed to take care of your needs. Right now you need to be in control. So as your Master, that is what I am going to give you. Control."

"Control? I admit I could use some. How do you propose giving me control?"

Nate's eyes were that soft blue she loved so much. He was always thinking about what she needed. Yeah, she knew that this was part of the Dominant in him. He was protective and giving. A stunning combination in any man, but in this man, it was devastating.

Nate rolled over and placed his hands over his head and grabbed the headboard.

"You may do as you wish to me, Mistress."

Holy shit! Had Nate just said that?

"Um, Nate. Are you sure about this? You said you were a Dom all the time. Doesn't this go against the grain a little?"

"Part of training to be a Dom is learning to submit, Bri. When I was training in LA, I trained with a Mistress. It is truly the only way to know how it feels to be spanked, paddled, whipped, on your knees. I will be truthful. I hated every fucking minute of it. I am not submissive by nature, so it was a real struggle for me. But it gave me a real appreciation for what submission means. I told you that part of my job is to give you what you need, not just what you want. Tonight is one of those times. You need to be in control, and I can give you this. Why wouldn't I?"

Could she do this? Take control from Nate? Even lying there he radiated command. But he was right. She did want to feel like she had control of things. What better way than to take control of him?

Brianne gave him a mock scowl.

"Well, I am going to be difficult to please tonight. You will need to obey me without question. Is that clear, slave?"

Nate's mouth twitched. She could tell he was trying not to laugh.

"Yes, Mistress. The slave will obey."

* * * *

Brianne was almost heady with power. Nate lay on her bed naked as the day he was born, with his arms above his head, gripping the headboard. He was laid out like the yummiest buffet she could ever imagine. It was such a luxury to be able to touch him however and wherever she wanted. Normally her hands were restrained and she longed to run her hands over his smooth biceps, his muscled back, his beautiful cock when they were making love.

She hardly knew where to begin. She swung her leg over and straddled his thighs. It was really the only hope she had of holding him down, other than restraining him outright. She could tie him hand and foot to the bed if she desired. She knew he would allow it, and he had installed discreet restraints on this bed that tucked under the mattress when not in use. But she wouldn't do that. Ultimately, this was about him giving her just enough control to feel better. She didn't need to tie him down and wouldn't take any more of this gift than she absolutely needed.

Knowing this was probably a one-shot deal, she decided to drag out the pleasure as long as she possibly could. She started at the top of his head, running her fingers over his short hair, inhaling his shampoo. It was a clean, citrus scent. She massaged his scalp before sliding her fingers down to his face. She took her time exploring his handsome face, running her fingertips over his stubbly jaw. He hadn't shaved since this morning. One glance at his white-knuckled hands told her that he was holding himself in check. His instincts were telling him to flip her off of him and take control. He didn't do it. She was overwhelmed at his love and control. She would never forget this gift.

Her fingers trailed down the corded muscles of his neck to his broad shoulders. She massaged those muscles until he groaned in pleasure. His cock was hard against the warmth of her pussy, and her juices drenched her cotton panties as she ran her hands over his gorgeous male body. She used her fingernails and scraped his nipples lightly, causing his body to jerk underneath her. Her fingernails stilled at the flat, male nubs, holding them in a gentle pinch. She could feel his cock pulse against her in reaction.

"Stay still, slave. I don't want to punish you." She tried to sound commanding. Nate must have practiced for years to sound as lordly as he did. One command from him and she was on the verge of orgasm every time.

Nate quirked an eyebrow at her words. "I'm sorry, Mistress. I don't want to be punished. If I misbehave again, what will you do?"

Well, shit. She didn't really know what she would do. This dominating stuff was harder than it looked. She would have to make it up as she went along. She wondered if he did, too.

"There's a drawer full of plugs right next to this bed, slave. You may find one inserted in you if you do not obey and submit."

Holy hell! Did she really just threaten her Master with a butt plug? Nate just looked at her with a sardonic smile. He didn't look very submissive, but then he really wasn't.

"I will obey and submit, Mistress. I don't want anything up my ass. I'm sorry."

She could tell Nate was trying to hold in his laughter. Apparently, she wasn't too damn intimidating. *Time to shut him up.*

"Silence, slave. You no longer have permission to speak. Now I am going to continue the inspection of my property, and you are going to lay here like a good slave. No coming without permission, either."

She lowered her lips to his chest and began exploring him with her lips and tongue. Her tongue ran down to his navel and then up to his nipples. She licked and sucked them until he was groaning underneath her. She nibbled a path down his rib cage and then up the other side, letting her hand trail down to his straining cock. He couldn't come without her permission. This would be fun.

* * * *

Nate gritted his teeth at Brianne's sensual exploration of his body. He was ready to come, right now, and she had barely touched his cock. He started reciting baseball stats in his head, holding off. Her soft hands had run all over his body and then when her lips and teeth had followed—Christ Almighty. It had been all he could do not to roll her on her hands and knees and ram into her from behind, showing her without a doubt who was in charge in the bedroom.

Instead, he lay there trying to be still and quiet as her tongue found his already painfully hard cock. He couldn't stop the moan that broke from his throat as she drew the mushroom head into the warm cavern of her mouth. He gripped the headboard harder in an effort to keep from tangling his hands in her auburn hair and holding her head there, fucking her mouth until he came. He wanted to shoot his load into her throat and watch her swallow his seed. Not tonight. She needed this.

He bit his lip until it bled and held himself still as her mouth and tongue started moving up and down, bringing him further into the maelstrom of pleasure. When she pulled off his cock with a pop, he groaned. He had never been close to begging before, but he was pretty damn close tonight. He opened his eyes to look into hers and saw them dark with passion. She was almost as gone as he was.

"My turn, slave. Keep your hands on the headboard."

Brianne scooted up his body, and he licked his lips in anticipation of what was to come. His little Mistress was going to give him a taste. He was surprised. After all this time, she should know that the one servicing was actually the one in control. But he wouldn't complain. Her pussy was a hairsbreadth from his mouth, and he could smell her arousal. The heady fragrance hardened his cock even more.

"Mistress, may I lick you?" Shit, even his voice sounded strained.

"Say please, slave."

She'd pay for that later, he thought. Teasing the mean Dom wasn't the best idea.

"Please, Mistress."

"Yes, slave. Make me come."

Yes, he would make her come, dammit. She would be begging before this was all over. He reminded himself that he had given control to Brianne. It was just one night.

Her fingers parted her folds, and he ran his tongue up and down her already-wet slit, learning every crease and crevice of her pretty pink pussy. He shoved his tongue as far into her entrance as he could, feeling her tight muscles hold him. He began to fuck her with his tongue and listen to her moans of pleasure. His hands unconsciously reached for her hips to hold her still on his face. She was too far gone to notice his breach of protocol. He shoved her pussy on his tongue in an effort to get it deeper inside her. He drew his right hand through her cream and trailed it back to her tight rosette. Using her own honey, he probed her tight little hole with his middle finger, fucking her ass with his finger and her pussy with his tongue.

"Oh God, Master, please! More, please! May I come?"

Ah, his sweet sub was ready to give up control. She was well trained and even on the top remembered to ask for her pleasure.

"Yes, slave, come for me now." He sucked her clit into his mouth and lightly scraped his teeth over it. He could feel her freeze above him and then her scream as she came hard. Her cream rained down on his face, and he licked and sucked at her pussy until she was limp above him.

"Are you ready for a good hard fucking, Brianne?" He rolled her on her back and looked down into her sleepy green eyes. She smiled and fluttered her lashes.

"Yes, slave. Fuck me hard."

Nate chuckled as Brianne switched to the top role. He snagged a condom from the bedside table before lining his cock up and slamming into her in one hard thrust. His eyes felt like they rolled back in his head as he felt her creamy, tight pussy hug his cock. It seemed to draw his cock in farther, and he pulled against the suction before allowing it to draw him back again. Over and over he fucked her hot, wet cunt. He rode her hard, thrusting to the hilt each time, bumping her cervix. She was keening under him, and through the haze of pleasure he could hear her urging him on. He knew he was close and reached between them to stroke her already-hard, sensitive clit. Two strokes and she was flying again. Her cunt clamped down on his cock, and he couldn't hold back the climax that seized him by the balls, turning him inside out. Sweat ran down his back as he plunged into her one last time before holding himself still as his cock jerked and throbbed his seed into the condom.

He held himself there as long as he dared before rolling over to dispose of the condom. He pulled Brianne's damp body next to his own, pushing her long hair out of her eyes.

"I love you, Brianne. There's isn't anything I wouldn't do for you."

Brianne's hand ran up his chest, and he felt his sensitive body quiver under her soft fingers.

"I love you, too, Nate. I can't believe that you did that for me. No one has ever done anything like that for me."

Nate tangled his hand in her long hair and tugged her face up to look into her green eyes.

"I would hope not. Do you have a stable of male submissives you haven't told me about?"

She giggled, snuggling closer to him.

"Nope. I think I will just stay your submissive, Nate. Being the dominant is way too much work."

Chapter 9

The lubricant tickled her ass crack. His fingers followed, caressing her back hole before pushing a finger in and electrifying nerves she never knew she had. His finger fucked her ass, and then he added another, fucking her harder, stretching the clamp-like muscles before adding a third. The pinch and burn made her catch her breath, and her juice gushed as her arousal was driven even higher. She had never wanted anything more than his cock in her ass right now. She wanted him to take her, fuck her, own her. She would have begged him to fuck her, but her voice wasn't working along with her lungs. She struggled to draw in a breath as he removed his fingers. She whimpered at the loss of contact. His impressive cock replaced his fingers, pushing at her tight hole. More cold lube was added, and then the head of his cock breached the ring of muscles. She groaned as he pushed forward relentlessly. His cock ran over the sensitive nerves, bringing her closer to orgasm.

"Really? It didn't feel like a gigantic tree trunk up her ass? And it felt so good she was speechless? I mean, slap me on the ass and call me Sally! That impressive cock probably was ripping her in two!" Noelle rolled her eyes at the passage they had been reading.

Lisa coughed as she laughed. "Dear Sally, anal sex with the right man can be an erotic, wonderful thing. It can feel really good."

Noelle shuddered at the thought. "No one is inserting a redwood in my ass, thank you very much. God gave my body an entrance and an exit, and I won't go confusing the two."

Tori was the logical one and pointed out a flaw in her logic. "What about oral sex? Technically, that is an entrance and an exit. Although it is a hell of a lot more fun as an entrance."

Noelle's mouth twisted with impatience. "I give head, if that's what you're asking. Although, if the guy doesn't reciprocate, then no deal. But you know what I mean by an entrance and exit. You know—down there."

Sara laughed. "Down there? What are we, twelve? You mean your pussy and asshole."

All the women groaned and covered their faces, shaking heads.

"Christ, Sara. Just because we read these books doesn't mean we have to use the words." Lisa laughed so hard she could barely get the words out.

Sara pulled a face and turned her attention to Brianne. "Going back a few sentences, and speaking of erotic and wonderful, how are things going with Nate?"

Brianne blushed a little at the turn the conversation had taken. No one really needed to know that she had taken down her entrance-and-exit signs for Nate. Her body was his unrestricted playground.

"Just fine, thank you. Taking a survey?" Brianne answered primly.

"Oooo, defensive. Good sign. You must be getting laid good these days. I remember those days." Sara's new baby boy was just a few months old and keeping her up almost 24/7.

"You could say I have sex on a fairly regular basis." Brianne tried to act nonchalant.

"Get real, Brianne. Nate gives you the high hard one pretty much every day, doesn't he? I assume that is why he never answers Conor's calls anymore." Lisa's eyebrows arched in question.

Okay, now she was really blushing. Nate was giving it to her at least once a day during the week and more on the weekends. He had turned her into a bona fide sex maniac. When she wasn't doing it, she was thinking about doing it or planning when they could next do it.

Nate had taken to using a gag on her so Kade wouldn't be woken by the screaming when she came.

"How much Nate gives it to me is no one's business but my own. But the management thanks you for your interest."

Tori tucked her feet under her and threw down her e-reader on the table.

"Seriously, Bri, sex life aside, how are things going with Nate? It would appear that you two are getting serious."

Brianne thought about the question carefully before answering.

"Well, yes, we are serious. Nate spends a lot of nights at my house, and Kade and I spend time with Nate and his kids, too. Nate tries to spend time with Kade playing games or shooting hoops. He has been great since Rick left. Nate is wonderful, but I don't want to rush him or make him feel pressured. I distinctly remember Nate saying it would be a cold day in hell if he ever got married again."

Nate's divorce from his high school sweetheart had started amicably enough. They had simply grown apart as the years had passed. But the proceedings had turned nasty when Jennifer didn't get everything she wanted in the divorce—namely the house, both cars, a boat, a vacation home, their investment portfolio, and lifelong alimony.

"Yeah, I remember that, too," said Lisa, "but you need to remember that Nate said that in the heat of the moment during a nasty divorce. From what I can see, you two sure act married. All that's left is someone saying some magical words over you guys and you can fight about in-laws and mortgage payments."

"We would never fight about in-laws. I love Conor and Nate's parents. You do, too, Lisa."

"Yes, but it has never stopped us from fighting about them."

Brianne chuckled as she pictured Lisa yelling about her in-laws and Conor threatening to spank her.

"Well, I am working on the assumption that Nate doesn't want to get married again. It's fine. I don't need to be a wife to be happy. I am happy with Nate right now. I don't want to spend my time wishing for things that I don't have."

She still felt badly for not telling him about Rick, that he had heard it from Lisa. She needed him to know she loved and trusted him more than anyone else. As long as he believed that, marriage was not a priority.

"Have you heard anything about Rick? Have they found him?" Sara asked.

"No. Sam says it looks like he picked up a pile of money from his Cayman accounts, and he and his boyfriend disappeared after that. He probably is traveling under an assumed name now. I don't think he's coming back. I know that Kade is hopeful. I walk a fine line between dashing all his hopes and allowing him to have some hope. Nate has been invaluable helping me with him."

In truth, Brianne loved having Nate around. It felt wonderful to feel like she wasn't on her own all the time. She didn't have to handle everything all by herself. They were a team. She had never felt that way with Rick. Rick had paid lots of attention to her until they got married. After that, it was his job to become a successful restaurateur. Everything else had been her job.

Lisa's eyes narrowed, and her mouth thinned in anger. She had never liked Rick in the first place.

"There's a special place in hell for Rick, and if there is any justice, it won't include lubricant."

Tori laughed, and it completely transformed her usually sad features.

"You want Rick to be rended anally? Is that even a word—rended? Isn't this where the conversation started? What happened to erotic and wonderful with the right man?"

Lisa's mouth twisted. "Let's just say I hope his new boyfriend is hung like a horse and only tops. Can I get an 'Amen'?"

All the women in unison shouted, "Amen!"

Brianne glanced at the clock. It was time to pick up Kade from day camp. This was his last week. Thankfully, school would be starting next week.

"As much fun as talking about asshole rending has been, I need to pick up Kade."

The others nodded in agreement, gathering their belongings and making plans for next week. Brianne had awesome friends.

* * * *

Brianne looked around the crowded playground for her son's familiar face. Kids were running around in the August heat, swinging on swings, hanging on monkey bars, and tossing basketballs. Brianne wiped at the sweat on her neck and frowned as she scanned their faces for her son.

"Brianne, what are you doing here?"

Brianne turned at the familiar voice of one of the day camp counselors.

"Hi, Nancy. I'm here to pick up Kade. Is he inside? I don't see him out here."

Nancy looked puzzled.

"Well, he already left. He left with his dad."

Brianne's mouth hung open in shock.

"Rick was here! Nancy, Rick is wanted by the police. If he was here, I need to let them know."

"No! I meant that Rick's wife picked Kade up. I didn't actually see Rick. It was his wife."

Brianne fought to keep her anger in check.

"Why was Tami allowed to pick up Kade? She's not on the list of authorized people. Only Rick and I are authorized."

Nancy's smile faltered.

"Well, Tami is Rick's wife. I just assumed she was helping him out today. I didn't think it was a big issue. Is this a problem?"

Brianne gritted her teeth to hold her anger in check.

"Yes, Nancy. This is a problem. There is absolutely no reason for Tami to be picking up Kade. For all I know, Rick called her and she is winging her way out of the country with my son in tow. There was a reason I never authorized her to pick up Kade. I need to call the police, and then I need to speak to your director."

Nancy's face was ashen with the full import of Brianne's words. Brianne had always liked Nancy but couldn't feel any sympathy at that moment. If Tami was taking Kade to Rick, there would be hell to pay. Brianne pulled out her cell phone and started dialing Sam.

* * * *

Brianne sat in rush-hour traffic on McMullen-Booth Road, trying to control her anger and panic. Sam had assured her they would put out an Amber Alert for Kade immediately. He was going to go to Rick and Tami's home personally to search as soon as they had hung up. The police were searching the area airports in case Tami was trying to take Kade out of the Tampa Bay area. They had also dispatched officers to question the staff at the day camp.

After her call to the police, she ripped the director of Kade's day camp a new asshole. If they hadn't allowed Tami to leave with Kade, this wouldn't be happening. The director had obviously been worried about a lawsuit and had frantically tried to find paperwork that authorized Tami to pick up Kade. Brianne knew they would find none. Brianne had been adamant that Tami not have Kade on her own. She didn't feel that Tami was responsible enough. At the time, Rick had given her a token resistance but eventually gave in. She had always secretly suspected he felt the same way.

Brianne had also called Nate and left a message. She didn't want him to think she didn't trust him to help her through this. The fact was she needed him right now. She was trying to be strong, but it was getting harder by the minute.

Traffic inched northward, and Brianne was relieved to finally get to the Tampa Road exit, head toward her neighborhood, and pull into her garage. Sam had said the best place for her would be at home in case Tami brought Kade there. He would send a police officer to stay with her. If Tami did show up there with Kade, it was going to be all she could do not to kick Tami's ass from here to Orlando for putting everyone through this.

Brianne walked into the house and checked the answering machine. No messages. Her cell phone was eerily silent, too. She walked into Kade's bedroom. It looked as it always did. LEGOs and action figures everywhere. The bed was barely made and shoes were scattered on the floor. Brianne lay down on the *Star Wars* bedspread and breathed in her son's familiar scent. She finally allowed her tears to fall. This was a fucking nightmare. The thought that she might never see her son again was too horrible for her mind to process. She choked back sobs and clutched at Kade's pillow.

She didn't know how long she lay there crying until she heard her cell phone ringing. Nate's ring. She ran to answer it.

"Nate!"

"Oh my God, Bri. I just got your message. Tami took Kade? What the fuck was she thinking? I'm leaving the hospital now, sweetheart. Are you at the police station?"

Brianne felt numbed as she shook her head then realized that Nate couldn't see her.

"No, I'm at home. The police said I should be here in case Tami brings Kade here."

"I'll be there as soon as I can, honey. Just hang in there. I'm going to call Lisa and see if she can come sit with you until I get there."

Brianne knew that at this time of the day it would take Nate at least an hour to get from the hospital in the southern part of the county all the way to Palm Harbor. Tampa Bay was famous for its traffic jams and terrible drivers.

"Okay, please drive carefully. I'm okay."

But she really wasn't, and she could hear it in her own voice.

"No, you're not, Bri. And you don't have to do this alone. We're all here for you. I need to hang up now, honey. I'm in some nasty traffic. I'll be there soon."

"Bye, Nate. I love you."

"I love you, too, baby. Hang in there for me."

Brianne sank back down on the bed and tried to calm her breathing. Was it only a few weeks ago that Kade had come home happy from his time with Rick and Tami? She remembered Kade's excited face as he had described fishing off the boat and catching the biggest fish of all.

The boat! Brianne sat straight up on the bed. Her heart went into overdrive, almost pounding its way out of her chest. *The fucking boat!* Tami could have taken Kade to that damn boat and sailed away by now. Brianne knew that was where they spent almost every weekend as long as the weather was good.

She would call the police and Nate from the car. She grabbed her purse and keys and headed toward Clearwater Marina.

Chapter 10

"Brianne, you need to wait for us. We are almost there. Do not search the boat by yourself."

Brianne pulled into the Clearwater Marina and put her car in park.

"They could be leaving now, Sam. I can't wait for you or Nate. I have to get my son back."

Brianne hurried along the grayed and weathered docks toward Rick's beloved boat *The Impetuous*.

"Shit, Brianne. This could be dangerous. What if Tami is armed?"

"I'm not going to just hop onto the boat, Sam. I will check things out. But I need to make sure the boat is here first then see if Kade is there. Oh, hell, the boat is there!"

Brianne felt some relief seeing the boat in its familiar slip. At the very least, Tami hadn't spirited Kade away via the Intracoastal.

"Okay, good, Brianne. Just sit tight. We're almost there. Traffic is a bitch, but we're just down the street."

Brianne barely heard Sam's voice as she caught sight of Kade fishing off the side of the boat. Relief swept through her body, and she sagged against a wooden pole as she drank in the sight of her beloved son.

"He's here, Sam. Kade is on the boat, fishing. He's okay!"

"Stay there, Brianne. We'll get—"

Brianne pressed the "end" button on her phone and dropped it in her purse. When she had spied Kade she had also seen Tami. Tami in a tiny pink bikini, drinking a Corona while lying on a chaise lounge. Just that quickly, relief was replaced by burning anger. Anger at Tami for putting her through the last few hours. Her spine stiffened, and her mouth thinned. *One ass kicking coming up.*

* * * *

Brianne climbed up the narrow gangplank and stepped over the railing of the boat. Kade heard her and turned from his fishing, dropping his pole with a clatter.

"Mom! I'm hungry!"

Kade flew to Brianne, and she hugged him tightly. Oh God, she had thought she might never see him again. She hugged him again as he began to squirm.

"Hey, Mom, you're squishing me! Are we going to get some dinner? I'm hungry."

Brianne kissed the top of Kade's head and pulled a granola bar out of her purse. She was always prepared for Kade's ravenous appetite. Tami sat up from the chaise lounge and peered at her through oversized white sunglasses. Brianne couldn't tell Tami's mood, but she didn't give a shit anyway. She was pissed off as only a mother could be.

"Eat this to tide you over until dinner, baby. Now go down the gangplank and wait on the dock for me. Some friends are going to meet you."

Brianne knew that the police and Nate were right behind her.

"He has to stay here, Brianne. He can't leave." Tami's girlish voice grated on Brianne's already-raw nerves.

Brianne gently pushed Kade toward the gangplank. She needed him off this boat. Now.

"He has to stay here!" Tami's voice held panic, and she started to rise from the lounge chair. Brianne placed herself between Kade and Tami.

"What in the hell are you doing, Tami? You kidnap Kade from day camp and bring him here? For what? He is so fucking not staying!"

Tami halted at the anger and command in Brianne's voice. If Brianne had learned anything these last months with Nate, it was that a certain tone of voice could get into someone's head. She needed that advantage right now. She needed Tami to listen to her.

"He is not staying here, Tami. He never should have been here with you. Why did you kidnap him?" Brianne put as much dominance and command into her voice as she could. It seemed to work, as Tami's shoulders slumped.

"He has to stay here," Tami whined. "He is the only thing that will make Rick come back."

"Rick is coming back? Has Rick called you, Tami?" Brianne kept the steel in her voice.

"No! I haven't heard from him, and he needs to come back! I need him here to take care of things."

"You cannot go around kidnapping people, Tami. I didn't know where Kade was. I was worried."

Tami frowned behind the owlish sunglasses.

"I didn't kidnap him. I just picked him up and brought him here. If Rick comes back, it will be to Kade and the boat. So I brought him here."

Brianne reined in her anger and kept her voice strong.

"If you take someone without permission, that is kidnapping. Did you even feed him?"

Tami pulled the sunglasses off, and Brianne could see tears in the other woman's eyes.

"There was no food here. Rick always took care of that. Rick needs to come home and take care of things again."

Brianne pressed her fingertips to her temples. This time it was Tami giving her a headache.

"I'm going to lose the house if Rick doesn't come back. Rick took all the money."

"Then get a fucking job, Tami. Rick isn't coming back, for God's sake. He's gone. He was an asshole to me and an asshole to you. You are well rid of him, if you ask me. Move on with your life. Sell the house, the car, and your wedding ring. That should give you a new start on your life."

Tami looked at her as if she was insane.

"Rick promised me I would never have to worry about anything ever again. He promised. When he comes back, he will look for Kade, and Kade will be here with me. Kade has to stay here with me. Rick loves Kade and the boat. He said so all the time."

Brianne shook with anger at Tami's asinine logic. This woman thought only of herself.

"Men lie, Tami. Rick was one of the worst liars. He lied to me, to Kade, and to you. Rick loved Rick. Maybe in his own way he loves Kade, too. But I can assure you that he didn't love anyone else. If he did, he sure as hell wouldn't have done this."

"He'll come back. He'll come back for me and Kade."

Tami moved toward the gangplank as if to go after Kade, and Brianne's thin hold on her temper snapped. She reared her fist back and clocked Tami right on the jaw. The woman went sprawling on her bikini-covered ass with a comical expression of shock.

"Shit, Tami, I didn't want to hit you. But you will never go near Kade ever again. Do you understand me?"

"Quite the right hook you have there, slugger."

Brianne rounded in surprise at the sound of Sam's voice. He was climbing over the railing along with two uniformed officers. The officers helped Tami to her feet and cuffed her hands behind her back.

"She was going after Kade, Sam. I had to stop her." *Oh hell, was she going to jail, too?*

"I know. I saw it all. Nate's down there, by the way. He's got Kade."

Brianne felt the breath whoosh out of her in relief. Kade was okay, and Nate was here. She ran to the railing and looked over to see Nate carrying Kade piggyback as her son ate his granola bar. She waved at the men she loved. They both smiled and waved back. It was all going to be okay.

* * * *

Brianne gazed at her son's angelic face as he slept. She was relieved to have him home and tucked up safely in his *Star Wars* bed. She was also sad that events had taken the turn that they had. Rick would miss out on his son growing up, falling in love for the first time, going to college, becoming a man. She winged a prayer upward that she would live a long life so she could be there for all those milestones. She wanted to be there for Kade.

It had been one hell of a day, and she was exhausted. She still couldn't believe what had happened, and she had spent the better part of the evening recounting the events for Lisa and Conor.

"So, are you pressing charges, Bri?" Conor had asked.

Nate had sat with her and rubbed her tense shoulders.

"Yes, I am. If she had been sorry, maybe I might have backed down. But she refused to see what she did was wrong. Maybe this will help her see beyond herself for a change."

"You did the right thing, Brianne. Tami needs to start taking responsibility for her actions. I'm just glad to have you and Kade in one piece. Tami's a little worse for wear, but she'll be fine, too," Nate had teased.

"I must say, after punching Tami I do feel better. I abhor violence, but she pushed me when she messed with my child."

"Hell yeah," Lisa cheered. "No one messes with a mama bear. No one with any sense anyway."

She slumped against the doorframe and closed her eyes. All the adrenaline that had been coursing through her veins mere hours ago had drained away, leaving her limp as a dishrag.

"You're almost asleep on your feet, Bri."

Nate's voice rumbled in her ear. She could feel the rise and fall of his chest as he pulled her into his arms. She burrowed deeper into his chest, pretending to snore. Nate laughed and swung her up in his arms, heading for the bedroom. She should protest that she didn't need to be carried, but she was honestly too tired.

Nate lowered her gently to the bed and began to undress her. She sat quietly while he efficiently stripped her shorts, shirt, and bra. She smiled when she saw that he pulled one of his old T-shirts out of a drawer for her to wear to bed.

"Arms up." Obediently, Brianne raised her arms over her head so that Nate could tug the Rays shirt over her head. She would need to buy him a new one next time they went to a game. She wasn't giving this one back.

"Lay down, sweetheart. Everything looks better after a good night's sleep."

She lay down and curled up under the light blanket. Before she knew it she was asleep.

* * * *

Brianne's eyes fluttered open, and she waited while they adjusted to the dark. A glance at the nightstand showed that it was five in the morning. Nate must have felt her stir. She could feel his body tense next to hers.

"You okay, Bri? Do you need anything?" Nate's voice was rough with sleep. She felt bad that she had woken him up.

"I'm fine. I slept like the dead but seem to be pretty awake now." She pushed to a sitting position and groaned as her muscles protested. She must not have moved the entire night.

"I think I almost feel human this morning. Thank you for taking such good care of me last night. It was so wonderful to have someone to lean on. I'm not used to that."

Nate pushed himself up also and flicked the bedside lamp on low.

"Good. Now we need to talk about your punishment."

Brianne froze as Nate's words penetrated her sleep-numbed brain.

"Punishment? What the hell have I done to be punished? I don't deserve to be punished!"

Nate's eyebrow quirked up in question.

"Are you sure? Did Sam and I both tell you to wait for us on the dock? Did we both tell you not to engage with Tami? You could have been hurt or killed. Tami might have had a weapon. I cannot allow you to take your safety for granted in this way. You need to stay safe so you can be there for Kade."

Nate's voice was soft but firm, and she felt a flush of anger at his reference to Kade.

"That's a low blow, Nate. My number one priority is Kade and his safety."

"Yes, his safety but not your own. You need to make your safety a priority, too. Kade and I want you to be around for a long time. I hope you want that also. You have given me no choice but to punish you."

Brianne's mouth hung open in amazement. Nate was totally serious. He was going to punish her for the harebrained move of boarding that boat without him or the police. *Wait.* Did she just admit it was harebrained?

Shit. Yes, it was a stupid move. Tami had been in a bikini, so she didn't have any concealed weapons, but that didn't mean that she didn't have any on the boat. The sheer stupidity of what she had done suddenly hit her. She felt tears leaking from her eyes.

His fingers captured her chin and turned her to look into his soft blue eyes. He had a gentle smile on his face.

"What's wrong, Brianne? This certainly isn't the first punishment for you, and if I'm guessing correctly, it won't be the last."

She scrubbed her hands across her face.

"The sheer stupidity of what I did yesterday just hit me. Fuck. She could have had a gun or a knife. I could have been hurt. Who would take care of Kade? You should punish me. I fucking deserve it. Drive some sense into my head, Nate."

"First of all, I would take care of Kade if anything happened to you. I love Kade like my own son. Secondly, the only thing I'm going to drive into you is my cock in a few minutes. I will decide your punishment later. But it is clear that you need me to make sure you don't do this again. That's why I have decided to marry you."

Marry her? His face appeared serious in the dim light. But he couldn't be serious. He didn't really want to get married. Did he?

"What do you say, Brianne? I think we should get married. Will you marry me and make us a family?"

Brianne swallowed the lump that had formed in her throat. Her eyes blurred with tears.

"Nate, what are you doing? I know you don't want to get married again. It's okay. I don't need to be your wife. I love you no matter what." Her voice was barely a whisper, but she knew Nate had heard her from the grin that spread across his face.

"Who says I don't want to get married? You're not thinking about something stupid I said while I was getting divorced, are you? I want to marry you, Brianne. I love you. I want us to be a family. Will you marry me?"

Brianne smiled at Nate and nodded, only to have him quirk an eyebrow at her.

"What's rule number one, Brianne?" His whisper was so soft, but she heard him clearly. *Oh yes, no nodding allowed.* He needed to hear her voice.

"Yes, Nate. Yes, I will marry you. I love you." She launched herself at him. They were going to be a family, and she was going to be punished. Her body was already starting to become aroused at the thought.

"Um, about that punishment, Master…" She nipped at his bottom lip and let her hands slip down his torso to stroke his already-hard cock.

"Yes, little slave, your punishment starts now." Nate grinned and pressed her back on the mattress, covering her body with his warm, solid weight. She gazed up into his handsome face and saw all the love she had dreamed of finding. Nate had been worth the wait.

THE END

WWW.LARAVALENTINE.NET

ABOUT THE AUTHOR

I've been a dreamer my entire life. So, it was only natural to start writing down some of those stories that I have been dreaming about.

Being the hopeless romantic that I am, I fall in love with all of my characters. They are perfectly imperfect with the hopes, dreams, desires, and flaws that we all have. I want them to overcome obstacles and fear to get to their happily ever after. We all should. Everyone deserves their very own sexy happily ever after.

I grew up in the cold, but beautiful plains of Illinois. I now live in Central Florida with my handsome husband—who's a real, native Floridian—and my son, whom I have dubbed "Louis the Sun King." They claim to be supportive of all the time I spend on my laptop, but they may simply be resigned to my need to write.

When I am not working at my conservative day job or writing furiously, I enjoy relaxing with my family or curling up with a good book.

For all titles by Lara Valentine, please visit
www.bookstrand.com/lara-valentine

Siren Publishing, Inc.
www.SirenPublishing.com

CPSIA information can be obtained at www.ICGtesting.com
Printed in the USA
LVOW04s1703140615

442438LV00022B/838/P